W9-CNA-859

Higgins Hole

Higgins Hole

KEVIN BOREEN

Illustrated by David Clark

 Charlesbridge

Published by Charlesbridge
85 Main Street
Watertown, MA 02472
(617) 926-0329
www.charlesbridge.com

Library of Congress Cataloging-in-Publication Data
Boreen, Kevin.
Higgins Hole / by Kevin Boreen; illustrated by David Clark.
p. cm.
Summary: The sea creatures of Higgins Hole, led by Petronius the sea horse and Lutus the lobster, defend their ocean home from a pack of three great white sharks, led by the infamous Tacitus.
ISBN 978-1-57091-641-0 (reinforced for library use)
1. Sea horses—Juvenile fiction. 2. Lobsters—Juvenile fiction. 3. White shark—Juvenile fiction. 4. Marine animals—Juvenile fiction. 5. Coral reef animals—Juvenile fiction. 6. Friendship—Juvenile fiction. 7. Coral reefs and islands—Juvenile fiction.
[1. Sea horses—Fiction. 2. Lobsters—Fiction. 3. White shark—Fiction. 4. Sharks—Fiction. 5. Marine animals—Fiction. 6. Coral reef animals—Fiction. 7. Friendship—Fiction. 8. Coral reefs and islands—Fiction.]
I. Clark, David, 1960 Mar. 19- ill. II.
Title.
PZ7.B6484Hi 2012
813.6—dc22   2011003474

Printed in USA
(hc) 10 9 8 7 6 5 4 3 2 1

Illustrations done in pen and ink
Display type and text type set in Goudy Old Style
Printed and bound September 2011 by Worzalla Publishing Company in Stevens Point, Wisconsin, USA
Production supervision by Brian G. Walker
Designed by Susan Mallory Sherman

To Kirsten and Stephen

Prologue

Why all the celebrating, you ask? We're thrilled because we've just saved our homes—indeed, our very lives! The fight for Higgins Hole was a great victory, probably the greatest in the history of the oceans.

What? You haven't heard the news? Jumping conch shells! Have I got a tale for you!

But first allow me to introduce myself. I'm a *Hippocampus erectus*, more commonly known as a sea horse. My name is Petronius. I was named by the great Lutus himself, an honor bestowed in our aquatic realm only upon those whose service rises above what's expected of a common fish.

You might not know I was named just to look at me, for, as Lutus points out, true greatness lies beneath one's scales. And yet you might suspect in passing that I swim a bit apart from the school. Doubtless you've noticed the elegant taper of my snout, which rises at the end in a noble cast. Many comment on my lovely translucent skin. The smooth facets of my body convey an air at once strong and refined. Fish of culture and taste have noted the tight coil of my tail, suggesting an easy grace at the dance.

But enough about me . . . Welcome! Our aquatic paradise, Higgins Hole, is located just a few days' swim off the Florida Keys. A beautiful reef encircles us, protecting us from storms, powerful ocean currents, and noisy ships. The reef pokes its rounded tops above the waves, which splash about them in a continuous, delightful whisper. Inside our reef the whitest sand lies beneath the bluest water, and no artist could equal the brightly colored tapestry of our coral. And there in the very center of the circle, as you can see with your own eyes, is the abyss, a depression in the seafloor so deep that no light has ever reached its bottom.

Although the origins of our abyss are unknown, theories abound. Lutus has speculated during lighter moments that it might have been dug by an enormous clam, though he's also expressed more serious possibilities. For example, he proposed to the Academy that a flaming rock from the sky might have hit the sea and penetrated deep into the sea bottom. He later suggested an alternative theory that a volcano had once existed here, exploded with immense force, and left this seemingly bottomless crater. This caught on as the Big Bang theory and is now much in vogue among our fish-a-cists. Whatever the truth of this matter, our fathomless abyss has always been a source of pride. And until yesterday, only Angie the Anglerfish, our esteemed oracle, knew its hidden secrets.

But look! Here comes Angie now. As word of her approach spreads, every sea creature stops its grazing to gather around the rim of the abyss. From here we can see everything and, better yet, everyone can see us. Don't be nervous. Act cool and casual. Firm the belly, twist the tail slightly, and, yes, perfect!

Angie completes her slow, stately ascent, her light shining ever more brightly from the splendid pod that extends from her shiny black forehead. Her large mouth, bristling with long yellow teeth, slopes back from her nose at a severe angle, stopping just below her ancient gills. It's been said that no other fish can survive where Angie lives, and—

Well, excuse *me!* A very large tuna just sent me spinning with a careless flip of her pectoral fin.

"I would think," says the tuna in the unmistakable warble of Miss Tootoo, "that a young sea horse such as yourself would have the sense to gather in the sea-horse section. Can't you see that Angie is about to make an announcement?"

"Indeed I can," I reply indignantly. "But I believe that you are the one who is out of place, Miss Tootoo."

"My goodness!" she says, lowering her nose to stare at me with her large green eyes. "Is that you, noble Petronius?"

"Indeed it is," I sniff. "And where else would I be but here, in my designated place, ready to perform my duties?"

"Well, of course, tiny Petronius, but surely you appreciate that a tuna of my stature must leave a bit of a wake."

"I barely noticed it," I say drily (which is not easy to do in the sea).

Miss Tootoo bats her eyes. "I'm often told that the smooth, delicate lines of my torso blend the waters behind me most gracefully."

"Your shape is much commented upon, Miss Tootoo," I concede tactfully, pinching one of my fins savagely to keep myself from saying more.

"Why, thank you, Petronius," she says with a titter. "My, you know how to flatter a tuna! But of course, what would one expect from our poet laureate? But please *do* be careful where you hover. I daresay you can't be but a billionth my size."

"If that, Miss Tootoo. But I must point out," I inform this cannery's dream, "with all due respect, that we are above the center of the abyss, and the center is reserved for—how do I say this?—*named* fish." Out of the purest consideration, I refrain from pressing the point, which is that she is not named, and indeed her self-declared nom de fin of Miss Tootoo is a scandal throughout Higgins Hole. Of course, no one would ever dream of taking her name away. As Lutus often says, "Better to be in the sea than in the skillet," and while we often wonder what this means, it's commonly understood that at times it's wise to let well enough alone.

With an upward thrust of her nose, Miss Tootoo takes her leave, her pectoral fins gently drumming the water by her side to avoid sending me cartwheeling into the coral.

Meanwhile Angie has reached our depth and stopped in the luminous blue water. Her pod shines dully as she rests, adjusting to the reduced sea pressure. These trips are exhausting for her, but as everybody knows, duty is her life, and we are the happy bene-fish-iaries.

We all wait expectantly around the circumference of the abyss, our great aquatic amphitheater, to hear what she has to tell us. The excitement shows in every mouth, fin, and tail.

Now, you have to understand that Angie's visits have always played an important role in our community. While her appearances are irregular, her declarations are usually the major topic of discussion for many tides afterward. Recent announcements have included:

"A hurricane's coming. Stay deep." (Good call, Angie!)

"There will be an earthquake tonight at five o'clock." (Not a big deal, though some crabs were badly shaken.)

"A fishing boat's on the way. Don't bite anything that doesn't answer back!" (We lost a good mackerel that day.)

"Just checking." (What a sense of humor!)

"Listen to Lutus." (And we always do.)

And, of course, it is Angie herself who announces which of our citizens is to be named, a task that falls to our dear Lutus, who always selects something just right.

Speaking of named fish, here they come!

There's our general, Integritus, a magnificent sailfish over ten feet long. Injured in our recent struggle, he bears his wounds with quiet dignity. His sharp bill juts forward like a steely saber. His large blue eyes, so expressive of courage and honor, convey an indomitable martial spirit.

Next to him is Apollo, an ancient sea turtle some believe to be more than three hundred years old, older even than Lutus. Apollo's reputation for wisdom and patience extends far beyond our waters. As our fish of state, he is often called to distant waters to settle disputes and arrange alliances.

Ah! And there's Harry the Herring. A droopy, long-nosed fish with a voice that can be as loud as a tanker's foghorn, dutiful Sheriff Harry shows the difference that even the tiniest of our citizens can make. Indeed, it was at Harry's naming many tides ago that Lutus declared, "Harry is living testimony that what matters is not the size of the fish in the fight, but the size of the fight in the fish."

Agamemnon, Achilles, and Hector, three enormous hammerhead sharks, swim in wide, lazy circles around us. (Don't worry, friends: they're charming.) The "Wide-Eyed Three," as we affectionately call them, have repeatedly risked tail and fin to protect us, and not even a mussel objected when Lutus conferred full citizenship upon them, proving that sharks can indeed lie down with clams.

I won't trouble you with my own accomplishments, nor with my duties as poet, witness, and historian, which, as Lutus kindly attests, immortalize us all.

Others have joined us, but Lutus is about to speak. I promise to introduce them to you later—splendid fish, all of them.

Do you see him? Look over there! He's mounting the white Speaker's Rock at the rim of the abyss. Yes, that's him! Have you ever seen a more marvelous lobster? Have you ever gazed upon more immense, encrusted claws or more finely tapered legs? His shell is the most beautiful shade of cordovan, a blend of reds and browns mellowed with age. His splendid black eyes perch above a small mouth from which I've never heard an unkind or foolish word. The gray whiskers and feelers around his face show the burden of leadership in peace and war, crumpled and broken from constant worry, but nonetheless alive, energetic, and, yes, even playful—a lobster in touch with his inner crustacean. Where would we be without him? What horrors would have been visited upon us without his leadership, his courage, his unshakable will, and his complete lack of shellfishness? But wait . . . he speaks!

"My fellow fish, mollusks, and annelids," Lutus begins in his deep, sonorous voice. "Distinguished named ones." (That's me!) "Join me in welcoming our dear friend Angie, who has ascended from the depths of the abyss to make an announcement."

A thunderous round of bubbles erupts from millions of open mouths, and none is larger than Miss Tootoo's, whose enormous belches topple several codfish onto their backs and create a bit of a skirmish in the fish-of-stature section.

Angie bows her head modestly, her pod bobbing forward so that it droops below her protruding lower lip. (Her best look, in my opinion.)

"What message do you have for us today, kind Angie?" Lutus asks, expressing the question tingling behind every set of gills.

"The time has come for a naming ceremony,"

Angie says simply, her tone and diction that of an aristocratic ladyfish. Amid another thunderous barrage of excited bubbles, Angie approaches Speaker's Rock and confers quietly with Lutus. Throughout Higgins Hole every fish contemplates Angie's news, jaws opening and closing as the importance of this shocking pronouncement sinks into the collective psyche. Another naming!

"Prepare for a great feast," Angie says finally, "and my most hearty congratulations." As she sinks back into the inky depths, quiet murmurs grow steadily into a roar of animated speculation.

Who will receive this greatest of honors? A name! Will it be the garfish who warned us of the first attack by Tacitus, the leader of the great white sharks? Will it be the courageous flying fish who swam tirelessly to warn the duke, the duchess, and the others that time was running out? The more I think about what's happened and the part that everyone played, the more I realize that there are millions of deserving nominees. Soon every fish has a favorite.

Lutus looks out over all the excitement, smiles knowingly, and with a wave of his claw, climbs down from Speaker's Rock.

"Who will it be?" I ask, joining him.

"All in good time," he replies warmly, patting the rounded bonnet of a starstruck young clam. The clam blushes from the great lobster's attention and snaps her shell shut. When I look back over my shoulder, I see the silly clam open a crack to see if Lutus is still there.

I swim beside Lutus as he makes his way to his apartments, greeting all as he passes but never, ever shaking hands. Word has it that he has quite a grip, unusual in our society of fishy handshakes.

"Lutus!" I insist, breathless with excitement despite my regular daily exercise and magnificent physique. "You must tell me. It's . . . for, ah, my poem. Who's the lucky one?"

Lutus turns and smiles at me, his feelers relaxed as they slowly poke at the water between us. "Will it be only one, good Petronius?"

Only one? I'd never even considered the possibility of multiple namings. "There will be two, then?"

"Remember this, Petronius. The smallest among us can perform the greatest deed. Unfortunately it's in the nature of things that we see what is large and neglect what is small. That's a mistake we must never make again."

Well said, Lutus, for this gem of wisdom lies at the heart of our story, a tale I'll share with you now, starting at the beginning. . . .

Chapter 1

Great events often have small beginnings, and our crisis began with a field trip by a school of young spadefish to a particularly lush coral dome called Manta Head. Billowing up from the seafloor within our pink, protective reef, the nooks and crannies of Manta Head teem with the most succulent and delicious treats. From a distance, the black-and-white striped spadefish, gliding to and fro among the coral, were a picture of peaceful, communal living. But as Lutus has noted on more than one occasion, when you get close enough to a fish, inevitably you see the scales.

"You look stupid," one of the fish jeered at

another. The victim of her mean words was a small fish grazing a bit apart, outwardly identical to the others except for a small, colorful piece of shell she had set in her dorsal fin.

Our stylish little fish tried to ignore the insult, singing to herself in her haunting, beautiful voice.

"She thinks she's too good for us," one fish chirped.

"Too good for us, or good for nothing?" sneered another.

"Do you think you're an oyster?" chided yet another, staring at the small piece of shell in the little fish's fin as others gathered around.

"Maybe she wants to be a crab."

"She looks more like a barnacle, if you ask me."

"Maybe it just started to grow there."

"Ew!"

"Her mother must be a conch!"

"Maybe when the shell's fully grown, it'll cover her face and we won't have to look at her."

"I stopped looking at her tides ago."

"Me too!"

And so it went, a stream of taunts directed against a simple act of self-expression. I'm embarrassed to admit that before our recent triumph, being the same as everyone else had become the supreme virtue among most of the unnamed creatures of Higgins Hole, and nowhere was this more pronounced than among the school fish, where fitting in was enforced by millions of jealous peers.

What possessed our little fish to flee at that precise moment we will never know. I have had occasion to ask her several times, and even Lutus inquired. Her reply was simply, "I was upset," and that is all we know even to this day. But flee she did. Hiding her tears, stung by the harping of fish who should have been her friends, she swam past Manta Head, past the mighty ring of reefs, past the wide, sandy shoals that make our home a hazard to even the most skilled human mariners, and out into the vast, deep expanse of the ocean, where the seafloor slides down to cold, forbidding depths.

The passage of time usually cools the heat of our anger, and just so, our little fish's fury quickly subsided. As it did, though, she found herself cold, alone, and with only a vague sense of where she was. She saw that above the water's surface, the sun had almost finished its daily trek across the sky. She knew that before long it would extinguish itself in the western sea, where it would keep the water warm

16

until it reemerged in the east to turn the early sky red and make new clouds. This was the first time that she had ever been by herself. She longed for the comfort of her school and the warm, bright waters of Higgins Hole.

Little did she know that at that very moment the sharp teeth of destiny lurked below!

Chapter 2

Swimming at the head of his pack of great white sharks, Tacitus, the Scourge of the Atlantic, moved his massive tail back and forth in a smooth, powerful rhythm. His eyes seemed to burn like hot coals on each side of his enormous gray head, which was covered with white scars from countless fights with sharks, whales, and those most deadly hunters in the seas, humans.

We learned of this only later, of course, but weeks earlier, having eaten every single fish off the coast of Iceland, Tacitus had addressed his shark pack thus:

18

"Brother sharks, terrors of the deep, eaters of whales and seals, today we devoured the last known fish within a hundred miles of this cold and forbidding island."

The sharks grumbled hungrily as they swam slowly around Tacitus. While great whites are normally solitary creatures and like to hunt alone, they wanted food and Tacitus had their complete attention.

"I met with the representatives of the Northern Leagues. Each has told me that nothing larger than a pinfish lives in their home waters and that we would surely starve if we ventured into their seas."

"Lies," one of the sharks hissed.

"They want it all for themselves," complained another.

"We'll starve if we stay here," another whined.

"As I well know," Tacitus acknowledged. "But my eels tell me that much of what they say is true. The humans have eaten more than their share. We have no choice but to find new feeding grounds." He thrust forward with a sweep of his muscular tail. "Some of you have campaigned in the southern seas with me before. Julius, we hunted together off the Cayman Islands many seasons ago."

"A great feast," Julius agreed.

19

"And Hannibal," Tacitus continued, "do you recall how full our bellies were after we sacked the coastline of Saint Bart's?"

"How could I forget?" Hannibal replied hungrily. "There was a whale for every shark."

"A whale for every shark!" some of the younger sharks cried, and they began to sing:

> *There is nothing like a whale!*
> *Nothing . . . in . . . the . . . world.*
> *There's no meat 'tween head and tail*
> *that tastes anything . . . like . . . a . . . whale!*

"Oh, yes," Tacitus assured them. "We've lived in northern waters for so long that many of you think that ache in your stomach belongs there. Well, it's really the first sign of starvation. I promise you: in the warm waters to the south, there is food beyond your imagination. Not just whales, mind you, but dolphins, marlins, and tuna—all of them soft, slow, and weak."

"What about the sharks that already live there?" one of the younger ones asked.

"There's nothing in warm water that could stand against a single one of you," Tacitus growled. "Under my command you've grown lean, strong, and hard. You'll need that toughness now, sharks, for I'm proposing a migration, a swim of several months. We must begin while we still have our strength. To wait here is to die."

"Lead us," the sharks told him. "We'll follow you anywhere as long as we can eat."

And lead he did. It gives me shivers to think of it, but using his keen sense of direction, Tacitus brought his pack south along the coast of Spain and Africa and then west across the Atlantic. As they advanced the water grew warmer. And the fish! The sharks ate as they had never eaten before, stuffing their bellies and growing bigger and stronger every day. Sadly, it is the way of the sea that no matter how much we have, we always want more. So it was with the sharks, who would sometimes merely take a single bite from a fish before moving on to the next. Such bad manners were inexcusable, of course, for everyone knows that a good shark always finishes his skate.

And so, when Tacitus sensed the presence of our little fish and heard her sobs, he winked at the sharks on his flanks and climbed in wide circles, stopping just behind her tiny tail.

"Greetings, little fish," he said to her, speaking gently so as not to alarm her. "You look especially well fed. Where are your home waters?"

She turned slowly, expecting to see a helpful dolphin or kindly nurse shark but instead confronting the gnarled face of Tacitus, one of whose wedge-shaped teeth was bigger than her entire body. She opened her mouth to scream, but nothing came out, not even a bubble. Her jaw worked up and down in utter helplessness, her eyes wide with terror.

"Little fish, I was hoping you could tell us . . ."

With desperate flicks of her tail, the spadefish swam away with all her might, following the dimming light to the west.

Tacitus laughed so that his whole body shook. "She'll show us the way," he bellowed. "Julius! Hannibal! Come with me. I suspect that this little one will lead us to a bountiful table."

Chapter 3

Our little spadefish swam for her life, past the sandy shoals, past the pink coral reefs, past Manta Head, across the rim of the abyss, and straight into Lutus's cave beneath Speaker's Rock. There she lay, shaking like a salmon laying eggs. I happened to be visiting and saw the whole thing.

"I–I–I–I," she stammered, flopping about as if she had been thrown into the bottom of a boat. (*Disgraceful!*) The Flop, popularized by the pop group Fleetwood Mackerel, had recently become the dance rage among the younger fish. Though this one had not yet reached what we call the Mindless Years, not even the most hysterical of teens would have dared to flop in the presence of our beloved leader.

"Calm down, little one," Lutus said, crawling to her, his eyes wide with concern, his feelers outstretched. "You poor thing. What happened?"

"Shark!" she finally squeaked. "I—I—I saw a sh-sh-shark! It was so—so big!"

"But there are many sharks in these waters, little one," Lutus said. "The sharks are our friends. We share our plinkies with them so they're never hungry. They'd never dream of eating a little fish like you."

Plinkies, by the way, are our delicious plankton patties, seasoned with carefully selected seaweed and kelp. Not only do plinkies serve as a tasty addition to our diet, but sharks adore them, and according to the Great Treaty, they long ago agreed to forgo eating the citizens of Higgins Hole in exchange for a weekly quota of plinkies. Apollo negotiates the quota periodically in an amicable session, which often ends in spirited rounds of Bite the Turtle's Head, which Apollo endures with patient grace.

"These were bad—bad sharks! Bad sharks, Lutus!"

"Oh, come, now. How could you possibly know if a shark was bad?"

"His teeth were as big as—"

"And even if it were a bad shark," Lutus said,

24

trying to soothe her, "the Wide-Eyed Three would chase them away. No one in these waters would dare challenge Agamemnon and his two brothers. Why, each of them is over fifteen feet long. And teeth? Achilles lost one yesterday that was the size of my right claw."

It was then that a mysterious but respected character in our world, a sea snake named Allus Neckus, slithered his green head into Lutus's chambers.

"The child's telling the truth," Allus Neckus said. "My sources report a series of atrocities going all the way back to Iceland. These sharks are fish eaters of the worst kind." Allus flicked his tongue. "Higgins Hole is in great danger."

"Where are they now?" Lutus asked gravely.

"The pack is still in the deep ocean," Allus Neckus answered, "but three of them are on the way here. I came to warn you."

As Lutus gazed down at his powerful claws, I saw his jaw clench with determination. "Allus, I know this is a lot to put on your, ah, shoulders, but we need to know who these sharks are and how to make them leave. Our very survival may be in your, ah, hands."

"I'll do what I can." Allus Neckus dipped his head and slithered out.

No sooner had Allus Neckus left than Integritus thrust his sharp bill into the chamber, nearly impaling me. "Lutus!" said Integritus. "You must come immediately!"

Lutus frowned. Such an intrusion by his spirited general was highly unusual, and our spadefish, who had finally grown calm enough to speak, was now staring cross-eyed at the three-foot-long bill that had almost run us through.

"Forgive me, Lutus, but this can't wait," Integritus said. We all heard the urgency in his voice.

"What is it?" Lutus asked.

"You'd better see for yourself."

Lutus crawled over Integritus's bill and made his way to the cave's opening. There he stopped, his two claws falling slowly at his side. Directly before him, swimming in wide, easy circles, were the largest great white sharks any of us had ever seen. Two of them were at least twenty feet long—huge, savage meat eaters with thick, muscular bodies and row upon row of white, jagged teeth. And the third, with eyes as dark as the abyss itself, was a magnificent, scarred beast of twenty-five feet. Lutus, for all of his courage, swallowed hard when he saw him, for he had never encountered a more menacing creature.

"Lutus," said the soft, cultured voice of an old friend.

Lutus turned to see a sea turtle gazing at him with large green eyes. "Thank goodness you're here, Apollo. Who are these giants?"

"The big one could only be Tacitus, the leader of the pack of great white sharks I've been hearing so much about," Apollo replied with majestic self-possession.

"I thought that great white shark packs were usually led by females," Lutus said weakly.

Apollo nodded. "Tacitus's mother was separated from the pack years ago."

"How?"

"One hears only rumors."

"How sad," Lutus said.

"Yes," Apollo said, "sad for him and for the rest of us. Without the moderating influence of his mother, Tacitus has become a monster. He's feared throughout the Atlantic, for his hunger and cruelty know no bounds. I warn you, Lutus: he's a clever, dangerous predator."

"But why are they *here?*" Lutus asked.

"Perhaps we should ask them."

"And if it's to eat?" Lutus asked, looking to Integritus and me.

"Courage, my friend," Apollo said gently.

Lutus grew silent. The situation was so scary and overwhelming that I couldn't begin to think of what we should do. I wondered what was going through the mind of our leader. Sharks don't commonly eat lobsters, after all. Would he simply choose to hide in his cave until they left?

No, I knew him better than that. Lutus shook his tail with firm resolve and climbed onto Apollo's broad back. Then Lutus turned to me and said, "Will you swim at my side, Petronius?" At once inspired and afraid, I agreed.

Digging his pointed legs into the crevices of Apollo's shell, Lutus informed his friend that he was ready, and the three of us made our way toward Tacitus. The gigantic shark seemed to watch our approach with curious amusement. Lutus whispered, "We'd have to double our plinky production to feed these brutes."

"I suspect they are after more than plinkies," Apollo said quietly.

"That we will never allow," Lutus said, catching Apollo's meaning, though I had no idea how we could stop these creatures from doing whatever they wanted.

We stopped a short distance from the sharks, and Lutus, without the slightest tremor in his voice, said, "Lord Tacitus, I presume?"

"So you know my name," Tacitus purred as deeply as the engine of a supertanker. "How nice. Yes, I am Tacitus. And you are?"

"I am called Lutus, a friend to all who visit Higgins Hole."

"Greetings, Lutus." Tacitus then asked a question considered polite among bottom-dwelling sea creatures: "And what rock did you crawl out from under?" Tacitus might be a ravenous, flesh-devouring monster, but I noted that thus far his manners had been impeccable.

After pointing to his abode, as is the custom, Lutus said, "We've never seen such creatures as you." He glanced at Tacitus's companions. "You and your colleagues are magnificent."

"We've had whales here, of course," I offered, wanting to impress, "but aside from them . . ."

"Whales, you say?" Tacitus grinned. "We've come from the far north, and sadly we haven't seen a single whale on our trip. I happen to be a great admirer of the species. Do you happen to know if any are close by?"

Apollo cleared his throat. "Whales are uncommon in these waters," he said, giving me a look of warning. I had never heard Apollo tell a fib before, but I noticed that he had crossed his back flippers, and I suppose a fib is justified if you're trying to keep your friends from being eaten. "They've come by special invitation for fish shows, of course, but we haven't had one here for what, Lutus, five seasons?"

"Oh, at least that," Lutus agreed immediately, crossing all his back legs and two antennae besides. "It's quite a chore to fit them through the reef."

Tacitus looked at Lutus and then back at Apollo. "I see," he said, taking the measure of his two clever hosts before his eyes slid expectantly toward me. Feeling foolish for having mentioned whales in the first place, I did what comes hardest to me and kept my mouth shut.

"Tu—na!" Hannibal suddenly cried, his eyes wide with excitement. "Toooo-naaaaa!"

We all turned and saw Miss Tootoo. She was returning from gorging herself among the shoals and was letting her associates know in no uncertain terms what she thought of the red snappers who had recently made Higgins Hole their home. "It all goes

30

back to the family, you know," she was saying, the reef echoing with her operatic indignation. "Upbringing, that's the thing. Dreadful manners. And what would you expect? The fathers think of nothing but their chums. The fools will choke down anything that drags behind a boat. . . ."

She took no notice of Lutus, Apollo, or the visitors. In fact, she took no notice of anything but her own opinions, as was her habit, for what could be more important? Consequently she did not see Hannibal, who, with a mighty thrust of his tail, sped toward her, his cavernous mouth opened wide to reveal his daggerlike teeth.

"No!" Lutus cried. "Miss Tootoo! LOOK OUT!"

"Hannibal, stop," Tacitus called out lazily, casting a somewhat embarrassed look at Apollo as if to say, *Sharks will be sharks. What can anyone do?*

But our warnings were too late. We gasped as Hannibal's jaws closed around Miss Tootoo's midsection. She screamed in horror, and we prepared for the worst. But then she kept on screaming, and we saw with some relief that the enormous shark was having difficulty with his intended meal. He had, in fact, bitten off more than he could chew.

"Hold on!" Integritus cried, his mighty sail

extended to its fullest, most resplendent height. Swooping down in a blur, he slashed his bill deeply through Hannibal's tail. The shark gasped in pain, releasing Miss Tootoo, who shot away to the protection of the reef with the agility of a minnow.

Integritus then executed the most perfect tuck-and-flip I've ever witnessed, dropping his head, twisting his body, and thrusting his tail back, ready to propel himself forward for a follow-up attack. Hannibal, whose tail was already beginning to swell, turned toward him angrily, his eyes cold and hard.

While several fish had joined Miss Tootoo to tend to her wounds, millions of others had gathered around Lutus and Apollo to watch the coming contest with fascinated terror.

"Perhaps you'd like to try that again," Hannibal growled to Integritus.

Ever the gallant, Integritus replied, "Don't ask for a bill you can't pay!" Integritus burst forward like a comet, darting his sharp nose left and right as Hannibal tried to match his movements with his huge, heavy head. And then, when it appeared to the breathless onlookers that Integritus was going to swim straight down Hannibal's throat, the sailfish flipped onto his back, soared over the shark's nose, and poked Hannibal sharply in the tail in a brilliant *bill-de-fin*, a move invented and immortalized by the great French sailfish Jacques Couteau.

My own blood was up, and I could no longer keep myself from the fray. While Integritus turned, I cried, "Prepare to meet thy mako!" and down I plunged, covering Hannibal in savage nips from head to tail. Though the wounds were not immediately obvious, I assure you that no shark ever suffered such a rash!

Overwhelmed Hannibal retreated to Tacitus's side. The fish of Higgins Hole cheered with the wildest enthusiasm. While Hannibal tried to elicit sympathy from Tacitus for his wounds, Tacitus gazed upon Miss Tootoo with obvious desire. If sharks had tongues, his would have been hanging out.

"I think our guests have had enough for now," Apollo said quietly to Lutus. "Perhaps it's time to ease the sting of the sailfish's bill with the salve of diplomacy."

We all turned to noble Lutus, wondering what he would do.

Chapter 4

Bringing himself up to his full height, Lutus clicked his claws enthusiastically and addressed the three sharks thus: "Bravo, bravo! Kind behemoths, sporting sharks, skilled practitioners of fishmanship, we are honored by your visit to Higgins Hole, and we applaud the wonderful spectacle you have just afforded us. We are often visited by talented travelers such as yourselves, but very rarely have we been entertained by such expert jousting."

Hannibal looked at Tacitus, his eyes screwed up in confusion. "Huh?"

"He's letting us save face," Tacitus whispered, not noticing me hovering nearby in position to attack.

"Go along with it," he schemed. "Besides that tuna, there's enough food here for a few good meals, and I'm sure there are whales nearby."

"Whales?" Hannibal and Julius said as one.

"I can smell them," Tacitus whispered. "Don't alarm the lobster and his turtle. I'll do the talking." And then, more loudly so that all could hear, Tacitus said, "I thank you for your kind words, Lutus. The eloquence of your tongue surpasses even your good looks. And fish of Higgins Hole, I thank you for your hospitality, for we are indeed travelers, and it is a privilege to come across proud and noble fish such as yourselves after the deprivations of the cold sea. And I especially salute you, sailfish, for your daring and skill, for which we, as simple and plodding sharks, are clearly no match."

The quills in Integritus's sail rose, for he is an honest fish who despises false flattery, but out of politeness he said, "You're tired from your long journey, or I'm sure I would have fared worse."

"Nobly said," Tacitus said, "and nobly done. Lutus, we take our leave. We hope the morning finds you all well fed." With that, Tacitus swam away, his two companions following closely at his side, all of us marveling at their size.

"I didn't like the sound of that one bit," Integritus said. "There's an ocean of difference between *bon appétit* and being *well fed.*"

"Did you have to do a *bill-de-fin?*" Apollo complained, his soft green eyes taking on a harder look. "It is said that a shark mends a wounded pride by filling its stomach with a fool."

"That shark nearly made a meal of Miss Tootoo," Integritus replied. "I had to defend her."

As he spoke, I'm sure I saw the general blush, confirming a widely held belief that Integritus and Miss Tootoo were becoming Higgins Hole's most unusual couple.

"I'm afraid Apollo may be right, noble Integritus," Lutus said, "though I hope I would have done what you did had I had been in your scales."

I then recounted what I had overheard from Tacitus.

"These dangerous visitors are not to be trifled with," Lutus concluded. "We can only hope that Tacitus and his friends will change their minds and leave our waters."

Integritus lowered his eyes. "I hope I haven't endangered Higgins Hole."

"My dear friend," Lutus said, raising the sailfish's

sharp bill with the back of his claw, "you are the bravest fish I have ever known. You proved again today that you are our greatest hero. You saved Miss Tootoo from a serious mauling, or worse." Turning to me, Lutus then said, "And what you did, Petronius, was incredibly brave."

I nodded modestly, but my heart soared.

Allus Neckus slithered silently into our midst and made his report. "There are twenty of them, and they're just a few hours' swim from the outer reefs. I overheard Tacitus say he'll return at dawn."

"I feared as much," Lutus said, resting his chin on his claw.

"What will we do?" I asked.

Lutus's antennae twitched as he thought. Finally he said, "We'll have a feast tonight."

Apollo arched his brow. "Do you think that's wise?"

"We mustn't cause a panic," Lutus said. "Tonight we'll open the plinkery. Everything that swims or crawls will eat its fill. Then each of us must take as much food as we can back to our holes, caves, and crevices."

"You're preparing for a siege," Integritus noted, admiration in his voice.

"Until we're sure these beasts have moved on, I fear we have no choice," Lutus said. "Petronius, please get Harry the Herring for me. Once everyone's assembled, I'll make the announcement."

"I'll post lookouts in the shoals," Integritus offered.

"And I'll return to the deep ocean," Allus Neckus said quietly. "We'll need as much warning as we can get."

"Thank you," Lutus said to the great spymaster, who slipped away as quietly as he'd arrived.

Apollo said to Lutus, "You're absolutely convinced the sharks will return?"

"I think we have to assume that, don't you?"

Apollo said, "Then we can't keep the extent of the danger from our fish for long. When will you tell them?"

"Fear is the most destructive force in the world, Apollo. Fear alone has killed many a fish. What we imagine is usually far worse than what actually happens. The only thing that matters now is that we eat and have food in our hiding places. If the sharks return, everyone will know the full danger soon enough."

As Lutus spoke these wise words, I looked out

over our watery home. Countless fish were playing in tight circles or hovering near their favorite reefs, recounting the duel between Hannibal and Integritus. The younger fish, fins pointing this way and that in youthful enthusiasm, practiced clumsy imitations of the tuck-and-flip and the *bill-de-fin*. In the distance, young marlins and garfish snapped to attention as Integritus sent them to their guard posts on the shoals. Miss Tootoo could be heard loudly in the distance, alternating between describing the atrocious oral hygiene of great white sharks and the lovely gallantry of a certain dashing sailfish.

"You wanted to see me," said Harry the Herring. Harry floated patiently behind Lutus, his long, droopy nose lowered in his quiet, unassuming way. He wore his sheriff's starfish proudly behind his gills.

"Yes, Harry. Please summon everyone to a public hearing."

"A hearing?" Harry said.

"Yes, I'm going to announce a feast."

"For everyone?"

"Yes."

Harry's nose dropped even farther. "As you wish, noble Lutus."

Lutus understood, and smiled. "Just ignore the red snappers, Harry. The rhyming makes them feel clever. They can't help themselves."

"I know," Harry said with a sigh, swimming away.

"They really are quite intolerable," Apollo said.

"Yes," Lutus agreed, "but what can anyone do?"

Apollo simply nodded.

"So tell me, Apollo," Lutus said, his eyes taking on a merry glint, "do you think Tacitus meant it when he said I was handsome?"

"Did he say that?" Apollo asked, his large leathery flippers gently treading the warm water. "I believe what he really said was that you are even more well spoken than you are handsome."

Lutus laughed. "That could be saying very little, couldn't it?"

Apollo paused. "I certainly think you are one of the more attractive lobsters I've met."

Lutus laughed again. "That's high praise coming from a three-hundred-year-old sea turtle."

"Don't let it go to your head, old friend," Apollo said with a grin. "At my age, everyone looks good."

Chapter 5

While Lutus was busy planning the feast, I accompanied Harry as he swam from coral to coral announcing the public hearing. Though by all outward appearances a gentle, quiet fish, Harry is universally treated with respect by the creatures of Higgins Hole. This is not just because he is named, and not merely due to his lifetime of faithful service. It isn't just out of deference to his unassuming manner, which is considered in good taste among all creatures wet and dry. No, there is something more. Harry is trusted to always do the right thing, no matter what it costs him personally, and that makes him a very special fish indeed.

We rounded an outcropping of rock, and I noticed Harry's nose droop farther than usual. There, waiting for him in a vast school, were the red snappers. Oh, how merry they looked! How smug! How pleased with themselves! Thousands of orange eyes watched with barely restrained glee as Harry and I approached, and I prepared myself for the coming unpleasantness.

Harry stopped in front of them and said, "There's going to be a public hearing."

Their rapid-fire reaction went something like this:

"What's a public herring?"

"Harry Herring said there's to be a public hearing."

"The herring said a hearing's nearing."

"A public hearing for Harry Herring?"

"How daring!"

"Thanks for sharing, Harry Herring!"

And so it went, an unending stream of nonsense. Harry listened patiently at first, but as the snappers continued, they missed the slow flaring of Harry's gills, the upward rotation of his snout, the fire in his eyes, the scales rising on his back. . . .

"ENOUGH!" Harry bellowed. "I'M BEYOND CARING HOW YOU'RE FARING, SICK OF

JOKES ON HARRY HERRING, TIRED OF SNAPPER VOICES BLARING, AND YES, MY PATIENCE IS WEARING, SO UNLESS YOU WANT TO GET A TEARING, I SUGGEST YOU GIVE YOUR TONGUES A SNARING!"

The snappers stared back at him, astounded, until one of them said, "Wow, that was good, Harry. Are you part snapper?"

"He's one of us!" another cried.

"Well done, Harry Herring!" said another.

All of them applauded heartily, and much to Harry's chagrin, they followed him for the rest of that fateful day.

In time we came across Integritus, who had been swimming the perimeter of the reef, encouraging each marlin at his post. I left Harry and his entourage of snappers and joined the general, his bill held high as he surveyed the murky blue ocean.

"I haven't properly thanked you for your help with Hannibal," Integritus said.

I assured him it was nothing, but we both knew better.

Integritus has never been one for small talk, so we watched together in silence as a small blue whale carefully navigated the reef. The truth was that whales routinely visited our plinkery, a sort of undersea spa where our hardworking crabs cleaned their baleen. This arrangement with the whales was probably Lutus's greatest single achievement, and since it's important to our story, I'll take a moment to describe the scene.

As we passed overhead, the newly arrived blue whale settled down on soft white sand with a happy, contented expression on her face. Then she opened her mouth wide, allowing thousands of crabs to crawl over her baleen, the thin ridges in a whale's mouth that strain the water for plankton and the other things that whales eat.

Just as people need to brush their teeth to avoid cavities, whales suffer terrible "toothaches" if their baleen isn't cleaned periodically. Vast quantities of shrimp, krill, and other creatures are removed by our industrious crabs, leaving whale mouths fresh, clean, and minty.

As we watched, the crabs brought the cleanings to row upon row of clams, who used their mighty shells to compress the ocean's harvest into plinkies.

Larger crabs carried the pressed plinkies to a storage area deep inside the coral, and as we passed above it we saw, to our utter horror . . .

"MISS TOOTOO!!" I exclaimed, aghast. No fish had *ever* broken into the plinkery, and there she was, her ample cheeks bulging like two sacks filled with sea cucumbers.

"Great Oceans!" Integritus gasped. "What are you doing?"

Miss Tootoo looked up at us, her eyes wide. She swallowed the contents of her bulging cheeks with great difficulty. "Why, ah, hello, noble Integritus and, ah, Petronius." She paused and added with a little smile, "How are you today?"

I felt sorry for Integritus, torn as he was between his duty and his affection for our embarrassed snacker. He said, "Miss Tootoo, this really is too much—at this time of great peril, to find you plucking plinkies from right under our bills."

"But I only ate a few thousand of them!" she pleaded.

"Tsk, tsk," I said. It was an awkward moment, not least because I knew that Lutus was about to announce a plinky feast.

"What will Agamemnon, Achilles, and Hector

47

say when they find out that you've eaten their dinner?" Integritus asked.

"But I was afraid to go outside the reef," Miss Tootoo said, her mouth trembling. "I keep thinking of that terrible beast. I can still feel his teeth on my scales and smell his sharky slobber. You know I have to eat every minute of the day! I'm so sorry, Integritus. I was just so hungry, but I promise: no more plinkies. I'll find another way."

We watched Miss Tootoo for a moment, deciding what we should do. I glanced at Integritus and realized that we share the great gift of leadership, which is to see into the hearts of others. We looked into her downcast eyes, saw her pectoral fins hanging loosely by her sides, and concluded that she was sincere.

"All right, then," Integritus said, taking the very words from my mouth. "I'm disappointed, but I know you to be fish of your word—all of them—and I'm going to trust you. This never happened."

"Thank you, noble Integritus. I won't disappoint you again."

"I'm sure of it," he replied, knowing that nothing inspires trustworthiness like trust itself. He gently lifted her chin with his bill. "But come, my dear. Lutus has summoned Higgins Hole to a public herring—I mean a public hearing—and we shouldn't be late."

"I'd be honored to swim at your side," she said, stifling a belch that nearly sent me tumbling to the surface.

Integritus led the way back to the abyss, each of us contemplating the painful prospect of a long siege and the famine that might bring.

Chapter 6

We arrived as Lutus was ascending Speaker's Rock. Every creature of Higgins Hole had gathered around the rim of the abyss. As always at such times, my heart was in my throat. Lutus addressed us all as follows:

"Fellow fish! Crabs, clams, and conchs! Much beloved creatures of Higgins Hole! We gather this evening to honor heroic deeds."

Millions of eyes were fixed on him, and I inwardly shuddered, awed by the enormous responsibility that Lutus carried on his spiny shoulders.

"As most of you will have heard by now, today one of our citizens was attacked by a shark."

"No!" millions cried. Even though most had seen the attack, it is well known that small fish have very short memories, so they gasped again in shock, bubbles of outrage rising in tall columns as they relived the horror through Lutus's recounting of the tale. Everyone was indignant that a shark would bite a fish, for, as Lutus once explained to me, most creatures tend to assume that the way things have been recently is what is normal, and our friendship with the Wide-Eyed Three was anything but normal when it came to sharks.

"Please," Lutus said above the noise. "Please listen. It wasn't an attack by one of our sharks, of course, but by a clan of great whites that happened to be passing by. Integritus—"

I coughed discreetly, catching Lutus's eye.

"And Petronius," he added quickly, "fought them off, saving Miss Tootoo. In their honor, I propose a Higgins Hole salute."

Acting as one, all the fish of Higgins Hole, large or small, skinny or plump, scaled or slimy, bent their tails back over their heads and, with an extraordinary precision befitting a crack squad of the Drum and Buglerfish Corps, swished their tails toward Integritus and me in a snappy flourish. Overcome,

Integritus bowed deeply. I could see that my fellow combatant was deeply moved, his gills quivering with emotion. I hoped I appeared as dignified, though I may have pumped my fin a few times. I'm not sure.

Lutus continued. "In celebration of Miss Tootoo's survival, we will open the plinkery for an all-you-can-eat-or-carry-away feast!"

The fish roared their approval. Everyone has enjoyed a plinky from time to time, of course, and the more daring routinely sniff around while the Wide-Eyed Three munch their meals each night. Although the hammerheads make an effort to be polite, they are sharks, after all, and rather messy eaters, so there are always plenty of delicious scraps to be had. No one was more excited than Miss Tootoo, of course, who whistled shamelessly while she twirled an unfortunate eel above her head in celebration.

Just then, Agamemnon returned through the reef, followed by his constant companions, Achilles and Hector. The three of them are by far the largest and fiercest citizens of Higgins Hole, and even Integritus has always treated them with a friendly deference. When the other fish saw them, they quieted quickly.

It was one thing for Lutus to offer plinkies to everyone, but what would the sharks think?

"Welcome home, Agamemnon," Lutus called out to him.

Agamemnon approached Speaker's Rock with slow grace, his bright, intelligent eyes fixed three feet apart on his distinguished, bony head. Achilles followed close behind, then came Hector, Achilles's enormous younger brother.

"We had good hunting at Alan's Reef," Agamemnon told Lutus. "I'm sorry we're late for the public herring."

"Hearing," Lutus corrected him. "That's quite all right. You missed the excitement today. We were visited by three great whites."

Agamemnon's eyes opened wide, which, if you've never seen it, is quite a comical sight on a hammerhead shark. "Great whites? This far south?"

"Are you sure?" Achilles asked.

"Oh, we're quite sure," Lutus replied. "Integritus and Petronius saved Miss Tootoo from one of the big brutes."

Agamemnon bowed his head briefly to Integritus and then looked at me with an admiration that some might have interpreted as confusion. "I'm sorry we weren't here to do our part," the big hammerhead said. "I haven't had a run-in with a great white for many years. They're very dangerous. Even threshers and makos fear them."

Lutus cast a nervous glance at the millions of increasingly anxious fish who were listening now with gaping mouths. "Perhaps we could discuss this some other time. . . ."

"I could tell you many terrible stories," Agamemnon continued, oblivious to Lutus's concerns, for he is an accomplished raconteur and hard to stop once started. "Some of the tales are so horrible, so mind-numbingly gruesome, so gory—"

"Agamemnon, please—"

"But I suppose the most ghastly accounts are of a particular great white shark who is more myth than reality, a shark they call the Scourge of the Atlantic. Just be glad it wasn't him!" Agamemnon's eyes grew wide again as he lifted a fin. "He's a cruel warrior killer beast by the much-cursed name of Tacitus!"

A highly strung mackerel was the first to faint, and within seconds several thousand fish were floating upside down in a state of shock. Agamemnon looked up in surprise. "What did I say?"

"Tacitus was here today," Lutus told him.

"No," Agamemnon said in disbelief. He turned to Integritus. "You fought with Tacitus and lived?"

"Not Tacitus," Integritus was quick to correct him, "just one of his lieutenants."

I coughed into my fin.

Integritus graciously added, "And then Petronius finished him off."

Agamemnon gave me that special look again. I was suddenly seized by the desire to bare a fang, though I don't have one.

"We're afraid they may come back in the morning," Lutus told Agamemnon. A wave of whispers spread across Higgins Hole like ripples on the surface as each fish told his neighbors the frightening news. Lutus asked quietly, "Can we count on your help?"

Agamemnon turned to his left. "What do you think, Achilles?"

"We've eaten plinkies here for many seasons," Achilles drawled. "I've developed a taste for them. I say we fight."

"And you, Hector?"

"I've heard that the meat of great whites is a bit stringy," Hector said in his big booming voice, smacking his lips. "Let's show those cold northern fish what a good ol' southern shark can do."

"I think you have your answer," Agamemnon told Lutus. The big hammerhead grinned as he spoke, but we could see the steely resolve in his eyes.

Lutus, relieved, said, "We are truly blessed to have you among us, valiant hammerheads. I hope you'll forgive me, but just as you arrived, I'd announced a feast. If there's a siege, we may have to hide in our holes for days without food, so we've opened the plinkery." Lutus motioned for Agamemnon to come closer, whispering, "We might as well eat what we have. If the great whites come tomorrow, they'll try to take everything."

Agamemnon nodded his big head. "We trust you, friend Lutus, and we ate well today. Do what you must and we'll support you." Then he added for all to hear, "I'd rather have friends eat my plinkies than some good-for-nothing whale eaters."

Lutus turned to the crowd and cried, "Creatures of Higgins Hole! To the feast!"

No one needed to be asked twice. In a single whoosh the entire population of Higgins Hole rushed to the plinkery.

The feast that followed was unlike anything Higgins Hole had ever seen. Every fish ate heaping mounds of plinkies. For those who were too small to handle a regular portion, the Wide-Eyed Three graciously crushed them into bite-size morsels. Miss Tootoo, in a state of pure rapture and apparently fully recovered from the shark attack, treated everyone to a stirring rendition of "Stuffed to the Gills."

> *Can't help it, but I wanna*
> *chow down like a piranha.*
> *Don't stop me 'cuz I'm gonna*
> *be stuffed to the gills, baby.*
> *Stuffed to the gills!*

Many were impressed with her fine, strong voice. Someone noted that she could really hold a tuna.

Every living creature ate its fill, and then, stomachs bulging contentedly, they carried as much as they could back to their homes. The waters of Higgins Hole were redolent with the spicy tang of plinky juice, and the plinkery itself was as bare and clean as a shark's tooth.

We all slept well that night, for we were indeed well fed, but as Lutus had foreseen, it would be the last meal we would enjoy together for many days.

Chapter 7

Have you ever eaten too much and felt a little sick the next day? Well, imagine having eaten your weight in plinkies at a single sitting! I confess that even I had a bit of a paunch that morning. The effort of sucking in my belly was really quite exhausting. Only Miss Tootoo seemed to be in good spirits, lecturing passersby on the merits of a particular clam's plinky production or the delightful piquancy of a certain whale's dental detritus.

Integritus, who had missed the feast, looked tired, having patrolled with the marlins all night. I found him briefing Lutus and Apollo on the latest intelligence.

"Allus Neckus was able to sneak into a meeting of

the great whites last night," Integritus reported. He recounted the sea snake's full report with such clarity that we almost felt as if we, too, had been there among them.

When Tacitus returned from Higgins Hole, he found the rest of his pack in high spirits, playing a game of Tooth or Dare. In case you haven't spent much time with frolicking sharks, the game involves swimming in tight circles, chomping another shark's tail, and then having that shark guess who bit it. A wrong guess results in a free bite from all of the other sharks, while a correct guess results in a free round of bites for the guesser. Apparently, as they were playing, a particularly dull shark named Cicero made the mistake of nipping Tacitus's tail. Cicero was nearly bitten in half as a result.

"That's enough of your silly game," Tacitus growled at them, Cicero pouting with a *what-did-I-do?* expression. "I have important news," Tacitus continued, "and Hannibal's been wounded."

"I'll eat that sailfish for breakfast," Hannibal vowed, uttering other sharky oaths that Allus Neckus faithfully related in his report but that I, out of politeness, shall not repeat now.

"That bill of his would make a fine toothpick,"

Tacitus agreed, but he quickly moved to more important matters. Addressing his full pack, he said, "Friends, we will never forget this day, for we have found our new home, and its name is Higgins Hole."

"They have tuna the size of submarines!" Julius exclaimed.

"I could hardly fit my mouth around one of them," Hannibal told them. "And I would have filled my belly with her if a soon-to-be-ex-sailfish hadn't poked me in my tail." Hannibal tried to show off his wound, but the other sharks were too excited about their next meal.

"Take us there now!" one of the sharks demanded.

"Why wait?" said another. "Tuuu—naaa!"

"Show us this place, Tacitus," they cried.

"Not tonight," Tacitus said. "That lobster's smart. He knows they can't fight us. He'll feed everyone tonight and tell them all to hide. I say we let them spend a frightened night in their caves. By morning their hunger will drive them out. When that happens, we'll be waiting."

"And then we'll eat them all?" Cicero asked hopefully, clapping his fins in excitement.

"Yes," Tacitus said, "but that will only be the first course."

61

"What's left?" the sharks asked.

Tacitus grinned. "Higgins Hole's greatest treasure."

"What good is that?" Hannibal complained. "Treasure's just bait for humans, and when they come down in those cages it's so hard to eat them."

"I hate the tanks," another shark agreed. "They give me terrible gas."

"You're supposed to spit those out, dummy," Julius said, a blissful look spreading across his face. "It's hard to beat the taste of a human once you get through that plastic wrapper."

"Their bones give me a bellyache," said one of the sharks. "Give me a nice fat seal any day."

"Are you finished?" Tacitus's eyes narrowed dangerously. "I'm not talking about pirate treasure. I'm talking about shark treasure. I'm talking about whales."

"Whales!" the sharks cried. Some of the younger sharks broke into a chorus of the ever-popular "There Is Nothing Like a Whale," but Tacitus bared his teeth.

"Yes, whales," Tacitus said. "The ultimate shark food: warm, juicy, and dripping with fat."

"And whales don't even have toofies!" Cicero pointed out.

"Then how do they fight?" another asked.

"Some of them do have teeth," Tacitus replied, "but the biggest ones don't, and those whales are utterly defenseless against a pack like ours."

"But I didn't see any whales," Hannibal said. "That old lobster and his smooth-talking turtle said they hadn't seen any for many seasons."

"Yeah," Julius said. "Not since that fish show." He frowned and wrinkled up his nose. "When do we get to go to a fish show? I want to see a fish show!"

"Silence, you fool!" Tacitus commanded. He turned to Hannibal. "Couldn't you smell them?"

"Well," Hannibal said, his forehead lined with concentration, "that turtle was pretty stinky."

"Not the turtle. The whales!"

"I don't think I've ever smelled a whale," Cicero confessed, staying well clear of Tacitus.

"And I'm not just talking about any whales," Tacitus said, ignoring Cicero. "I'm speaking of blue whales, the biggest living creatures in the sea, and the most delicious. There's no smell in the ocean like blue whale," Tacitus said, his stomach growling. "Years ago my mother and I were hunting a pod of them off the coast of Chile. I was about to swallow one of the babies when its mother, one of the biggest blues I've ever seen, came up behind me and held me in her jaws while her child escaped. It was the last time I saw my mother, but I'll never forget the smell of that whale's baleen and the spicy scent of plankton and krill. I smelled it again tonight. Higgins Hole reeks of it! I'm sure there are blue whales there. And if that's true, our migrating days are over."

"We've found the Hole of Plenty!" Cicero exclaimed. "Just like it says in the ferry tale."

"That's *fairy* tale," Tacitus corrected him, his annoyance growing. "Listen to me. When the sun rises, we'll circle the reef and approach from all sides. Nothing will escape. Anything that moves gets eaten. Rest well tonight, my sharks. Tomorrow we feast on whales at Higgins Hole!"

Chapter 8

When Integritus finished Allus Neckus's report, Lutus looked up at us and said, "This is worse than I feared. Anything that moves . . . yikes!"

"I agree," said Integritus, shaking his head as everyone jumped out of the way of his sharp bill.

"Be careful with that thing," Apollo complained. "Being around you is like trying to swim across a crowded shipping lane."

Lutus walked to the edge of the rim and peered into the abyss for what seemed a long time. "Integritus," he said eventually, "pick your bravest and fastest swimmer and send him to me. I have a special mission for him."

"Is it dangerous?"

"I fear it is."

Integritus frowned. "Then send me."

"No, we need you here. You're our champion. The fish have confidence in you. Even Tacitus will have second thoughts after watching you in action yesterday."

"Who will you send?" I asked the general, ready to volunteer.

"There's a marlin in whom I have particular confidence," Integritus said. "I've mentioned him to you before, Lutus. He's young, but he has a brave heart, and he can swim as far and fast as any fish I've ever known."

"We'll need every bit of his speed," Lutus said.

Apollo looked at Lutus as realization dawned. "You're going to summon the Flying Dolphin Squadron!"

Lutus nodded. "I only hope they can get here in time."

"The squadron could help us, of course," Apollo said, "but the latest reports are that they're fighting a nasty pod of tiger sharks off Havana. It could take them days to get here."

"All the more reason to hurry," Lutus replied.

"We'll need to go to Oceanus to obtain a resolution from the Oceanic Council," Apollo added with a heavy sigh. "Enlisting the Flying Dolphin Squadron is no laughing matter."

"I'm counting on your help, Apollo. Oceanus troubles me. I know nothing of its ways."

"That's to your credit," Apollo said. "I've always thought you were too good for politics."

"If politics can save us from being devoured by sharks, then I'm all for it," Lutus said. "We have no time to lose."

"I'll send for the marlin at once," Integritus said, darting off toward the shoals.

"And what about the whales?" Apollo asked.

"We have to warn them," Lutus said. "The Baron and Baroness von Finbocker left the plinkery two days ago, so they're safe, and Allus Neckus managed to sneak out a small blue last night. No new whales are due for several days."

"Whom are we expecting?" Apollo asked.

"The Duke and Duchess of Aruba," Lutus said, clearly worried about his old friends.

"For all their great strength, the duke and duchess are no match for Tacitus and twenty great whites," Apollo observed.

"We'll get word to them somehow," Lutus said, slamming one claw into the other. "We simply *must* . . . save the whales!"

Chapter 9

Once again Lutus asked Harry the Herring to summon everyone to the abyss. Their sense of danger heightened and hoping for more plinkies, the creatures of Higgins Hole gathered unusually quickly. There was an air of tension and dread in the sea. Even the snappers maintained a respectful silence.

Lutus had just climbed Speaker's Rock when a garfish swam up to him breathlessly. The poor fellow had been badly mauled, and I felt a pang of guilt that such a brave, selfless fish had no name.

"Lutus!" the wounded hero cried. "They're coming! The great whites! Just beyond Manta Head!" The brave fish had obviously risked his life to warn us.

His message delivered, he collapsed at Lutus's feet.

"We're under attack!" Lutus cried. "Someone help this poor fish, and everyone else go back to your hiding place! Don't come out until I announce that it's safe." Then, remembering why he had summoned everyone in the first place, he added, "Apollo and I are going to the Oceanic Council for help. Conserve your strength and your plinkies. Whatever happens, don't lose faith. We shall return!"

The fish looked back at Lutus in a state of shock and disbelief. Hadn't Integritus defeated Hannibal the day before? Weren't Agamemnon, Achilles, and Hector—not to mention a certain very lethal sea horse—ready to protect Higgins Hole? Lutus had never left Higgins Hole before. How would we survive without him?

But there was no time to debate. The hulking form of Tacitus appeared from behind Manta Head. At first he was just a huge, dark presence in the sea, like an approaching ship. But now we could see the scars on his cruel face. And this time, not two but twenty great whites followed him. Tacitus scowled, thrusting his heavy head left and right, searching for food. Clearly he meant business.

"WHERE ARE THEY?" he bellowed.

"Who?" Lutus asked, standing his ground bravely atop Speaker's Rock, gesturing with his extended claws for us to disperse. I helped the wounded garfish into Lutus's apartment while Harry the Herring ensured a smooth flow of traffic, reminding everyone to conserve their food, offering helpful hints about concealment, and settling occasional disputes when multiple fish converged on the same hiding place.

Tacitus was too hungry to notice the rest of us. "I smell whales. Tell me where you're hiding them!"

"I don't see any whales," Lutus said innocently. "Do you, Apollo?"

"Whales?" Apollo looked left and right. "What would a whale be doing here? You know, they're terribly difficult to hide."

Lutus looked back at Tacitus and shrugged. "See? No whales."

"You're lying," Tacitus said. "I smell plankton and krill. We've circled the reefs and shoals all morning. The scent is coming from here. You have whales inside this reef."

Lutus shrugged. "You're free to take a look."

"I can smell the BALEEN!" Tacitus roared.

"Oh, that." Lutus chuckled, though I could see that his back legs were shaking before the gigantic beast. The lobster's courage was astounding. "Now I understand," Lutus said. "You smell our plinkies. They're food pellets that we make from plankton. Would you like one?"

"Do you take me for a fool?" Tacitus growled.

One of the great whites swam up to their leader's side. "Tacitus!"

"Not now, Julius."

But Julius couldn't contain himself. "I think I know where the whales are."

Tacitus's eyes narrowed. "Where?"

Julius pointed a fin down at the abyss. Tacitus eyed it suspiciously.

"How deep is it?" Tacitus asked Lutus.

"No one knows," Lutus said, gazing down at the inky blackness. "An anglerfish named Angie lives down there, but to the best of my knowledge, only she can stand the sea pressure."

Tacitus turned to Julius. "Go straight to the bottom and tell me what's down there."

"Is it safe?" Julius asked.

"Are you a shark or a minnow?" Tacitus taunted.

"Well, a shark, I think—I mean, of course, but what was that about pressure? I don't know, Tacitus. I've never really done well under pressure. . . ."

72

Tacitus turned on him and revealed his razor-sharp teeth. "I promise you that the bottom of that abyss is the safest place for you to be for the next few minutes."

"Right." With considerable reluctance and a few nervous glances back at Tacitus, Julius descended into the abyss in slow, cautious circles. Soon he disappeared into the inky depths.

"You seem out of sorts this morning, Tacitus," Lutus observed.

"Nothing a few tons of meat in my belly won't fix."

"One should always start one's day with a solid breakfast," Lutus said.

"Perhaps this morning I'll start with a little tuna," Tacitus replied. "Where's the tender morsel that Hannibal gummed yesterday?"

Lutus took a step back. "You can't be serious!"

"I've never been more serious. Bring her to me, and we'll let the rest of you live while we wait for Julius to return."

"Why, that's barbaric!" I cried. "Are you suggesting that we offer up Miss Tootoo as a—as a *tunan* sacrifice?"

"That's exactly what I'm proposing." Tacitus

looked directly at me, and I must confess that my tail went slack with the thought that he might challenge me then and there. But then he looked past me, and a smile formed on his face.

"Why, look what we have here, Hannibal. The fancy sailfish returns."

Integritus swam toward them boldly, a handsome young marlin by his side.

"So you're back," Integritus said to Tacitus, glancing at the glowering Hannibal. The marlin, a splendid young fish with a blue star on his forehead, floated alertly by Integritus's side, his eyes fixed on the intimidating leader of the great whites.

"Indeed we are," Tacitus replied coolly.

"Tacitus just suggested that we feed him Miss Tootoo in exchange for our lives," Lutus informed them.

"Savages!" Integritus lunged forward, but Apollo intervened, moving between them. "Please, Integritus, control yourself. The word of the day is diplomacy."

"A hot temper is a dangerous trait in a commander," Tacitus observed, his eyes moving slowly to Hannibal and then back to Integritus. "Consider yourself fortunate that I have control of mine."

Just then, millions of gasps erupted from the reef,

and twice as many eyes were drawn toward the abyss. A pale shape was rising slowly from its depths. It was Julius, his body limp and drained of color. Hannibal and Cicero rushed to him, followed by Tacitus. Julius was still alive, but barely.

"He went too deep," Lutus said quietly. "What a shame."

"Can you hear me, Julius?" Hannibal asked, nudging his friend with his nose.

The poor shark's jaw moved slowly, but he was unable to speak. His eyes were bloodshot, and his skin was covered with circular white welts. Tacitus examined him carefully, and I saw a fleeting look of confusion cross the leader's face before he proclaimed, "It's pressure poisoning—that's all. He'll recover. I've seen this many times."

"He doesn't look so good," Hannibal said, lifting one of Julius's limp fins.

"Maybe a little nip would wake him up," Cicero offered helpfully. Every shark instantly volunteered.

"No nips," Julius groaned with considerable effort, flipping slowly back onto his white stomach. Some of his natural gray was returning, but he still looked awful. His eyes were mere slits in his head. He shivered.

"What did you see?" Tacitus asked him.

"It was so dark I couldn't see the end of my nose." Julius paused. A grimace formed on his face and quickly passed. "But I sensed . . . something. Something very strange and very large."

"A whale?" Hannibal asked hopefully.

"I don't know," Julius said. "I . . . I couldn't tell."

"Whales breathe air," Tacitus observed. "If it's a whale, it can't stay down there forever. We'll just wait here until it surfaces." Tacitus turned to Lutus. "In the meantime, we need to eat. If you know what's good for you, you'll turn over that tuna."

"And if I refuse?" Lutus replied.

"DO NOT TRIFLE WITH ME!" Tacitus roared, his patience gone. He propelled himself forward with a mighty thrust. Integritus leaped in front of Lutus, his bill pointed dangerously at Tacitus. But the huge shark was simply too powerful, and Integritus's brave gesture was as futile as a minnow attempting to hold back a wave. With a mighty toss of his head, Tacitus knocked Integritus off balance and snapped his huge jaws. The young marlin reacted just in time, shoving Integritus sideways so that the shark's razored teeth just missed the middle of the sailfish's body. But the center of Integritus's beautiful sail, the envy of every

76

fish in Higgins Hole, was torn lose and swallowed hungrily by Tacitus. The next bite would have killed Integritus, but the marlin, with complete disregard for his own safety, darted up and then straight back down, digging his stout bill into the top of Tacitus's head. Tacitus threw him off easily, but the marlin's quick, heroic action allowed Integritus to withdraw and save his life.

Tacitus had only begun to fight, however, and we saw firsthand that his fearsome reputation was richly deserved. Snapping his jaws ferociously, he rounded on the marlin, and only the athletic young fish's amazing reflexes kept him away from the flashing teeth.

"Help him!" Integritus cried, too wounded to move.

That's when Harry the Herring and the snappers swooped down on Tacitus, swimming circles around his head so fast that the big shark couldn't see through the churned water. Seizing my chance, I slipped into the melee and gave that brute a bite he'll never forget!

"To your caves!" Lutus cried, and a moment later all the creatures of Higgins Hole, including the herrings and snappers, were safely concealed.

The great whites thrashed the water angrily, looking for someone to attack, but we were safe for the moment. Tacitus charged a tight crevice where several tuna were hiding, scraping his nose painfully on the sharp coral. It only made him more furious.

"You can't stay in your holes forever!" he raged, swimming the circumference of Higgins Hole with powerful chops of his mighty tail.

Then the long, curving shapes of the Wide-Eyed Three appeared above, their bodies dark against the bright surface of the water. The hammerheads and the great whites saw one another at the same time. Both seemed to sense the danger, though our hammerheads were badly outnumbered.

"So it's true," Agamemnon said. "The terrible Tacitus is not a legend after all, but a real shark."

"Yes," Tacitus said, a strange, dark tone creeping into his voice. "And judging by your size, you must be Agamemnon."

"You and your associates are going to have to leave Higgins Hole," Agamemnon said, demonstrating nerves of steel. "Go back north where you belong."

"We like it here. I think it's unlikely that you or anyone else will force us to leave."

"Your size may inspire fear in other waters,"

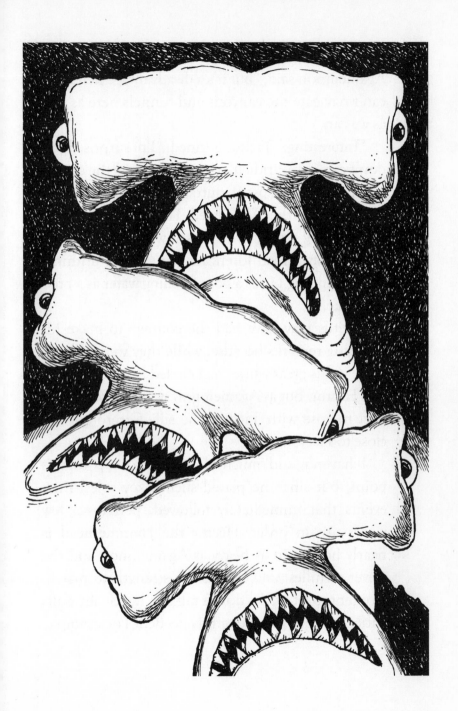

Agamemnon said, "but it's a disadvantage here. You can't navigate the canyons and tunnels here as well as we can."

"Interesting." Tacitus grinned. "I'm surprised you don't catch your ridiculous heads among the coral."

This drew gasps of outrage from every hiding place. While the Wide-Eyed Three are as slow to anger as any sharks I've ever known, to insult their, shall we say, broad foreheads is nearly as unthinkable as sending Lutus a pot of boiling water as a practical joke.

Tacitus may have had the courage to make his insulting remarks because, while they were talking, some of his great whites had circled behind Achilles and Hector. But as Agamemnon swam forward to go nose-to-nose with Tacitus, the silly Cicero got too close to Hector.

I haven't said much about Hector up to this point, but since he played such a key role in the events that immediately followed, perhaps a few words are in order. Hector the Hammerhead is nearly half again as heavy as Agamemnon and the clever Achilles, and he has the strength to match. Content to let others do the talking, he usually waits patiently until his strength is needed. For example, if a whale has to be nudged into position at the plinkery or a marooned fishing boat towed out of our waters, we send Harry the Herring to find Hector.

So when Cicero got within biting distance of Hector's tail, Hector glanced at Achilles, saw him wink, and smacked his tail into the great white shark's face, sending him howling to the surface and into the air.

The other great whites backed off immediately—all, that is, but Tacitus. Agamemnon, nose-to-nose with the enormous beast, showed no fear as they traded unseemly shark trash talk too rude to be included in my narrative.

Then it happened. With lightning speed, Tacitus surged left, throwing Agamemnon off balance, and then spun right, passing down Agamemnon's side and biting off the hammerhead's side fin in a single chomp! Noble Agamemnon uttered not a word, but it was clear to all that he was seriously wounded. Agamemnon tried to counterattack, but with just one side fin he could only swim in circles. Tacitus, who seemed to know exactly what he was doing, bore down on Agamemnon to deliver a lethal bite, but Achilles and Hector intercepted Tacitus and fixed their jaws around his back, biting with all their might. Tacitus cried out in agony, and the other great whites, smelling blood in the water, raced into the fray.

The sea was so full of enormous thrashing sharks that I couldn't tell what was happening. None of us had ever seen anything like it! I longed to sink my teeth into our attackers, but Lutus held me back, fearing I'd be crushed between the writhing bodies. It soon became clear, however, that our hammerheads were seriously outnumbered. They wouldn't have survived if that brave marlin, the one with the blue star on his forehead, hadn't soared above the fight and shouted, "I'll warn the whales!"

"Follow that fish!" Tacitus roared, throwing off the badly wounded hammerheads. He and the great whites, some slowed by their injuries, swam after the marlin as he led them away from Higgins Hole, and thus the fight ended as quickly as it had started.

Chapter 10

The creatures of Higgins Hole streamed from their caves, crevices, and concealments, swarming around Integritus and the valiant, wounded hammerheads. Lutus followed on Apollo's back, his face a picture of worry, for the great whites would surely return, and the hammerheads were now too badly hurt to help us.

In the confusion I was the first to see a dim light ascending from the depths of the abyss.

"Look!" I cried. "Angie's coming!"

Miss Tootoo, understandably terrified, peeked out of her cave. Having heard every word of Tacitus's demands, she had all but resigned herself to being eaten, and now, the immediate crisis having passed, she shook with rage and terror.

Apollo brought Lutus to Speaker's Rock, where he waited for Angie, who seemed to be rising with unusual speed.

"Angie," Lutus said when the anglerfish arrived, the oracle's face puffy from the rapid ascent, "it's too dangerous for you to be here. Tacitus may return at any moment."

"That marlin was very brave." Angie's pod flowed up and down, her lower lip protruding with fierce determination. "No act of such selfless courage should go unrewarded."

"Is the marlin to be named, then?" I asked.

Angie nodded. "And quickly."

"Just a moment," Lutus said, scrambling down Speaker's Rock and disappearing for a moment into his cave. I wondered what he was doing, but he returned promptly to his position atop the rock. "Then let him be known to all as Blue Star," Lutus said, "and may he return to us safely to know our gratitude."

Every fish bubbled its approval, for all had witnessed and marveled at Blue Star's selflessness and courage.

"There will be a siege," Angie said, her expression unusually grim. "With apologies to Agamemnon and his friends, the Wide-Eyed Three are no match for these great whites. Higgins Hole will endure great suffering. Each and every one of you, like Blue Star, must show courage. If you stay in your hiding places and keep hope alive in your hearts, you'll survive and laugh again. Help will come."

"We're going to send for the Flying Dolphin Squadron," Lutus told her. "Meanwhile I'm going to plead our case before the Oceanic Council."

"As you wish." Angie nodded sadly and turned back toward the inky depths. "True help is a rare thing in the sea."

The fish turned their eyes to Lutus. Higgins Hole had never known a time of suffering. Under Lutus's gentle claw, we had always lived amid peace and plenty. Facing the unthinkable, we set our fears aside and placed our faith in Lutus, a leader who had earned our trust through countless acts of virtue and kindness.

"What does this mean, Lutus?" Harry the Herring asked, speaking for all of us.

"The sharks will either catch Blue Star or tire of following him," Lutus said sadly.

"They'll never catch him," Integritus said with the quiet pride of a father. "He'll make it."

"I certainly hope so," Lutus said. "Whatever happens, the great whites will return. These ravenous creatures spared us this time because they thought we were hiding whales. Now we've all seen what they're capable of. While they wait for the whales to come, they'll try to fill their bellies with as many of us as they can catch. That's why you all have to stay hidden until help arrives. And I promise you, help will arrive."

As I pondered Lutus's promise, I remembered what Angie had said, and I resolved that if anyone ever needed my help in the future, I would give it without question, whether they were named or not.

Suddenly we heard an exuberant roar from the farthest shoals, and the joyous outcry grew like a mighty tidal wave, gathering force as it approached. Every creature was caught up in it, and even the seaweed, normally oblivious to our enthusiasms, seemed to wave in greeting. All of Higgins Hole began dancing for joy, opening before the brave young marlin with a blue star on his forehead. The marlin swam straight to Speaker's Rock.

"I'm sorry I took so long, noble Lutus," the marlin said. "I led the great whites out to sea. They stopped to rest, but I'm afraid they'll be back soon." Having made his report, he looked left and right for his wounded commander.

All of our hearts swelled with pride, and I've never seen Lutus so moved. "Noble Blue Star," Lutus said.

The young marlin looked behind him, wondering whom Lutus was addressing. Like the rest of us, the marlin knew all of the named fish, and he had never heard of Blue Star.

Many laughed, but contained in the laugh was admiration for one so modest and humble, and yet so excellent.

"Much has happened while you were away," Lutus told him. "Angie paid us a visit and announced that you were to be named." Lutus's eyes glistened. "Henceforth all will know you as Blue Star the Marlin."

As the fish bubbled wildly, Blue Star, overwhelmed by the unexpected honor, pressed his fin against his breast and bowed, emulating the style of his mentor, Integritus, who looked on with pride. At that point Lutus stepped aside, and Integritus swam forward, making no attempt to conceal his mangled sail, which now had the profile of a suspension bridge.

"Blue Star," Integritus said, gazing down on him. "My Blue Star," he repeated more quietly. Integritus slowly touched his bill on the left and then the right side of Blue Star's head, the highest honor a sailfish can bestow, and without further words, for none were necessary, Integritus withdrew.

"Blue Star," Lutus said, "you have already done so much for us, but I have a mission for you."

"Speak it," said Blue Star, snapping to attention, "and it will be done."

"The Duke and Duchess of Aruba are due here in two days to have their baleen cleaned. They should be passing Cuba as we speak. Find them and warn them about the great whites. Then proceed to the waters off Havana and bring back the Flying Dolphin Squadron."

"The Flying Dolphin Squadron!" Blue Star raised his head. "Do you think *he* will be there?"

"Almost certainly," Integritus replied. Blue Star was referring, of course, to the most famous dolphin in the world, the daring, gallant, and ever so handsome Megamaximus Sharkbonker.

"In the meantime," Lutus said, "Apollo and I

must go to the Oceanic Council to obtain a resolution against the great whites. Hurry back to us, Blue Star."

"I won't fail you." Blue Star lowered his head, bent his tail over his head, and snapped off a salute, which millions of fish spontaneously returned in a heartwarming display of respect and affection. The crowd opened for Blue Star as he set off on his mission. Then we all returned our attention to Lutus.

"You heard Angie," Lutus told them. "You'll be safe in your caves and holes. Stay there until we return. It's you that will face the greatest challenge, for you must master your hunger and your fear. Remember that hunger is like a baby, crying to get what it wants. I've lived longer than most of you, and I promise you that your hunger, like a baby, will soon tire and muffle its complaints with sleep. With the blessing of the Oceanic Council, Megamaximus Sharkbonker and his Flying Dolphin Squadron will soon rid us of this scourge, and we'll all be safe and happy again."

"What can I do?" I asked Lutus, wanting to help in the most, well, visible kind of way.

"My able Petronius, did you think I'd journey to the council without my aide?"

At these words, I stood straighter, if such a thing is possible for a creature shaped like a question mark, hoping that everyone else had heard them, too.

Lutus turned to Integritus and asked, "Will you take my place while I'm gone?"

"No one could replace you, Lutus," the sailfish said, "but I'll do my duty."

"How long will you be away?" Miss Tootoo asked from her cave, still shaking.

Lutus looked to Apollo, who answered, "Perhaps two tides, Miss Tootoo. Maybe a little longer if we have to wait to make our appeal."

"Given the seriousness of our situation," Lutus said, "I'm sure that we'll receive an immediate audience."

Apollo cautioned, "The affairs of oceanic governance are often more complex than they at first appear."

"Then we have no time to lose," Lutus said. "We'll leave immediately."

And we did.

Chapter 11

Heartened by the cheers and best wishes of our friends, we started our journey to Oceanus. Lutus looked splendid, perched at the peak of Apollo's shell like an emperor on his chariot. I swam beside Lutus, which was easy given the speed of turtles, particularly those of the ancient variety. Apollo passed majestically across the dark center of Higgins Hole, past Manta Head, past the pink reefs and shoals, and into the gray-blue sea, his leathery fins plying the water with steady determination.

Lutus had many questions about Oceanus and the council, and Apollo was a wise and patient teacher.

"Since anyone can remember," he began, "the oceans have been politically split between two parties, the Little Fish Party, popularly known as the Minnows, and the Big Fish Party, known as the Tunas. . . ."

In their wisdom, the founding flounders knew that the Minnows would always win the popular vote by margins of hundreds of billions, and without the protection of a second chamber in the council, they feared that the Minnows would pass laws forbidding the consumption of little fish. Larger fish opposed this for a variety of high-sounding reasons, though the obvious one was never mentioned in polite company.

Accordingly, the great patriot Salmon Adams devised the bicameral Oceanic Council, which is not to be confused with a biclameral system, which is one in which two clams make all the decisions, the worst form of close-minded tyranny.

Thus for centuries we have had a Little House, which is dominated by the Minnow Party, and a Big House, which is dominated by the Tuna Party. Membership in the Tuna Party does not require one to be a tuna, of course, but by a long-standing rule one must weigh at least four hundred pounds to be sent to the Big House. This effectively restricts the Tuna Party to groupers, flounders, and, of course, tuna, although the rule has been challenged many times, sometimes colorfully so, as when a very popular herring tied an anchor to its tail prior to the weighing-in ceremony, claiming it as a natural appendage. He was promptly eaten by his intended colleagues, not the first to be consumed by politics.

While Apollo was a fascinating tutor, it wasn't long before Lutus noticed that our progress in education was vastly exceeding our progress over the seafloor.

"Is this as fast as you can go?" Lutus asked.

"I'm pacing myself."

"Well, full speed ahead!" Lutus ordered, bracing himself for sudden acceleration.

"Lutus, I'm going as fast as I can."

"All ahead flank!"

"My old flanks aren't what they used to be," Apollo complained.

Lutus sighed, but then he winked at me. "Petronius, would you mind pushing?"

Despite the anxiety we felt over our upcoming audience with the council, we laughed gratefully, for as Lutus often says, humor is the best tonic for adversity.

Many miles to the south, as he later recounted to me, the marlin newly named Blue Star swam with all his might. Repeatedly he broke through the water's silvery surface and rose high into the air, searching the sea for signs of the Duke and Duchess of Aruba.

Finally something caught his eye. He darted up again, leaping higher to get a better view. He saw it clearly this time, two big white spouts in the distance.

He had found the duke and duchess, and they were in great danger, for they were far closer to Higgins Hole than any of us had thought.

Blue Star flew like an arrow to the magnificent blue whales. He could not remember seeing larger ones. Their spouts shot a hundred feet into the sky, and their tails, as wide as a ship's beam, rose high above the sea and then thundered down like the crash of mighty waves against the shore.

"Good day, young marlin," the duke greeted Blue Star in his deep, rich baritone.

"Good day, sir," Blue Star said, noting that the whales spoke perfect Fish without the slightest accent. He nodded to the duchess respectfully. "Madame Duchess."

"And good day to you. What an attractive blue star you have on your forehead," she said, obviously pleased to be in the presence of a cultured and polite youth, rare in any species.

"Where are you bound at such speed?" the duke inquired.

"I was sent to find you," Blue Star replied, "and then I'm to go to Havana."

"Big ruckus there," the duke informed him. "The Flying Dolphin Squadron is finishing up some tiger sharks, you know. Pesky beasts, those tigers."

"Are they still there?" Blue Star asked excitedly.

"The squadron? I imagine so, old boy. I spoke with Megamaximus myself just yesterday."

"He's soooo good-looking," the duchess purred. The duke cast her an irritated glance.

"I'm on an urgent mission to find him," Blue Star said. "I'm from Higgins Hole . . ."

"Our favorite spa!" said the duchess. "We're on our way there now."

"A few days early," the duke noted. "You've got to love the Gulf current this time of year."

"You might want to reschedule your appointment," Blue Star said. "We've been attacked by a pack of twenty great white sharks, and they seem intent on eating whales."

"Great whites?" the duchess gasped. "At Higgins Hole? My dear!"

"Please be careful," Blue Star urged.

"I've dealt with great whites before," the duke said. "They are super-pesky. A rap or two with my tail usually sets them straight. But twenty of them! Gadzooks!"

"They're led by a brute named Tacitus," Blue Star told them.

The duke exchanged worried glances with the duchess. "That," the duke said, "is indeed bad news."

"We've encountered that scurvy scoundrel before," the duchess said, struggling to maintain her dignity in the face of remembered fury. "We should have brought him to the icy prison of Antarctica when we had the chance." She sucked in her lower lip. "He attacked one of my babies once. It was just too horrible. I had to hold that distasteful cur in my mouth while my little blue escaped. I still have nightmares."

"I trust your child escaped unharmed," Blue Star said.

"Oh, yes, and how thoughtful of you to think of

her." The duchess looked to her husband proudly. "Yes, she's fine now, fully grown to a hundred thirty tons and with a family of her own. She married into a fine family off Tierra del Fuego. Her husband's a very fine whale. A *blue* one, of course."

"We did manage to bring Tacitus's mother down there," the duke said. "Nasty business, that. Had to be done. Can't have one's babies being eaten, can we?"

"You've been most kind to warn us of Tacitus and his thugs," the duchess said. "Since our dental appointment at Higgins Hole seems ill-timed, perhaps we can help you find the Flying Dolphin Squadron."

"Thank you for offering," Blue Star said, "but everyone back home is hiding in cracks and crevices without food, so every minute counts. If you could just point the way, I have to reach Megamaximus Sharkbonker as soon as possible."

"I hope Lutus has thought to obtain a resolution from the Oceanic Council," the duke sniffed. "Rule of law and all that, you know. It's the way of the seas these days."

"Lutus is on his way to the council now," Blue Star said.

"Splendid, splendid. I daresay you look a tad faster

than us. Head straight south. At the rate you're going, you should reach the battle in just a few hours. You really can't miss it. Roughed-up sharks everywhere. The duchess and I will swim behind you. By the way, do you speak Mammal?"

"Why, no," Blue Star said, feeling foolish. "I'd just assumed that everyone . . ."

"Dolphins aren't fish, you know, old boy. Even we have trouble understanding them sometimes. But that Megamaximus Sharkboinker . . ."

"*Sharkbonker*, dear," the duchess corrected him, batting her eyelashes. "Soooo cute!"

"I can never keep their ridiculous names straight," the duke complained. "Anyway, he's quite a chap, and his Fish is passable. He's . . . What's the word I'm looking for, Duchess?"

"I believe it's peppy, dear," she suggested, adding dreamily, "and soooo—"

"Exhausting," the duke said, "that's what I say. Can't keep up with him. But a fine chap nonetheless. Reminds me of myself when I was younger."

"Oh, please." The duchess rolled her eyes.

The duke just smiled. "Well, off you go, marlin. Make your course due south, and we'll see you off Havana."

Chapter 12

Blue Star swam furiously, encouraged by the news that the Flying Dolphin Squadron was close by. Soon enough he began to hear the distant sounds of battle. The war cries of dolphins mixed with the *oophs* and *ughhs* of the tiger sharks as the dolphins hammered them with their hard noses. As Blue Star swam closer, the sounds grew more distinct. Now he could hear the cheerful chatter of the dolphins. Though he couldn't see them, they sounded so confident, so self-assured, so endlessly energetic, and so, well, *happy*, even in the face of the dreaded tiger sharks. Surely, Blue Star thought, the great whites would wither under the blows of these veteran and fearless shark fighters.

He swam even faster. Ahead, a large fish was approaching him head-on with desperate speed. It was a tiger shark! It was smaller than a great white, but still a fearsome beast. Blue Star summoned his nerves and positioned his bill to defend himself, but the dazed shark sped past him, not even taking notice. The dolphin in pursuit saw Blue Star and stopped, a broad, swaggering grin on its silvery face.

"Eh-eh-eh!" the dolphin said merrily.

"Excuse me?" Blue Star said.

The dolphin, his intelligent eyes smiling at the corners, turned his head to the side and repeated, "Eh-eh-eh?"

"Oh, I'm terribly sorry," Blue Star said, frustrated. He had no idea what the dolphin was saying. He suddenly wished they'd taught languages in his school. In desperation he asked, "Do you speak Fish?"

"Of course," the dolphin said good-naturedly. "What do you expect from the most intelligent animals of the sea? I'm not bragging, of course," the dolphin said playfully, executing a somersault. "That's just the way it is."

"It sounds like bragging to me," Blue Star replied,

a little put off, "and I wouldn't draw any conclusions about your relative intelligence until you've met our Lutus."

"Then meet him I shall," the dolphin said with a laugh. "But for the time being, I can speak your language and you can't speak mine, so I win!"

"I've never claimed to be a scholar," Blue Star said, "though when my training is complete, I'd like to become one."

"What are you training to be, marlin?"

"I want to be a defender of Higgins Hole, like my teacher, Integritus."

The dolphin stopped. "Integritus the Sailfish?"

"You've heard of him?"

"Of course. We're the most intelligent animals in the sea."

"Yes, you mentioned that."

"You're a good listener. You'll make a fine student. My name is Maximagnificent Sharkbanger. What's yours?"

"My name is Blue Star, though I haven't had it very long." The two of them politely wagged their fins at each other. After these pleasantries were exchanged, Blue Star added, "I'm here on an urgent mission, Maximagnificent Sharkbanger. I'm looking for Megamaximus Sharkbonker and the Flying Dolphin Squadron. Higgins Hole is under attack, and everyone may soon be eaten. We urgently need your help."

"Eh-eh-eh!" Maximagnificent Sharkbanger replied enthusiastically, doing a triple backward somersault. "Fresh sharks! Wonderful! Follow me! Eh-eh-eh!"

The dolphin blasted off with an incredible burst of speed. Blue Star, tired from his long journey, had to struggle to keep him in sight. Soon they were passing some of the most miserable sharks Blue Star had ever seen. Their stonelike faces stared into the distance as dolphins swam circles around them, slamming into any shark that so much as bared a single tooth.

Ahead of them Blue Star saw a dolphin floating upright on his tail with his fins akimbo, and he knew in an instant that it could only be Megamaximus Sharkbonker himself. He was a glorious creature—tall, lean, and dashing, with muscles on his muscles and a perfectly shaped nose that, though completely unscarred, looked like it could split a ship in half.

"Eh-eh-eh!" Maximagnificent Sharkbanger called out to his chief.

"Eh-eh-eh!" said the handsome leader of the Flying Dolphin Squadron, smiling down on Blue Star.

"Are you Megamaximus Sharkbonker?" Blue Star asked in awe, already knowing the answer. There could be no other dolphin like the one before him.

"I was this morning," Megamaximus Sharkbonker replied in perfect Fish, much to Blue Star's relief. "What brings you here?"

"We need your help, sir."

"And I'll be happy to give it. But call me Max. All the dolphins do. It's quicker. Quick is good. Quicker is better. Quickest is the best! Eh-eh-eh! An eel tells me that Tacitus has been foolish enough to leave the Arctic. Is it true?"

"Yes. He's waiting at Higgins Hole to eat our whales."

"Higgins Hole? Excellent! We're finished here. We've turned these tigers into catfish. They won't be bothering anyone for a while. We'll leave at once. You've got the Oceanic Council's resolution, of course? Can't go shark bonking without it."

"Lutus is obtaining the council's authorization as we speak," Blue Star informed him, adding honestly, "but I don't know if he actually has it yet."

"Apollo will know what to do," Max enthused. "And how is Lutus?"

"You know them?" Blue Star asked, impressed.

"Eh-eh-eh! Of course. We are, after all, the most intelligent animals in the sea." Max smiled and winked. Then he lifted his fin and let out a high-pitched squeak. The mighty Flying Dolphin Squadron, a hundred dolphins strong, gathered around him.

"What now?" a splendid dolphin, a little older than the others, asked with gusto.

Max winked at Blue Star. "Meet Superexcellent Sharkmasher, the sergeant major of the Flying Dolphin Squadron."

"Eh-eh-eh!" cried Superexcellent.

"How do you do?" said Blue Star.

Megamaximus Sharkbonker thrust his stream-lined, muscular body forward to address his eager squadron mates. "All of you, say hello to our new friend, Blue Star the Marlin."

"Eh-eh-eh!" the dolphins responded cheerfully.

"He's from Higgins Hole. It appears that Tacitus and his scruffy gang have decided to plant a fin there, intent on devouring our oversize cousins."

The dolphins laughed at Max's joke about

whales, who are indeed distant cousins of dolphins.

"Who gets the first thump?" Maximagnificent Sharkbanger asked.

"You know the rule," Max said with a laugh. "Whoever gets there first! And who will it be?" Max looked from one happy silver face to next. "Will it be you, Megastupendous Sharkwomper? Or you, Maxiterrific Sharkbasher? Or you, Superglorious Sharkzamboozler! You can't wait to slam your snoot into the underbelly of a great white, can you?"

"Eh-eh-eh!" Superglorious answered, spinning energetically in a tight circle.

"All right, then," Max concluded. "Let's go stick our noses into some sharks' business!"

Everyone laughed, wagging fins and fluttering tails.

"I don't know how to thank you," Blue Star said, overwhelmed as he was by these powerful, friendly dolphins.

"All in good fun," Max said, waving his fin as if to say that chasing away twenty great white sharks led by the most feared creature in the seven seas was just a matter of routine. "Tacitus will be a bit tricky, of course, but we love a challenge, and if you're not having fun, you're not doing it right." Max winked.

"Just make sure you get the council's approval, OK? Well, off we go!"

Wanting to be polite and knowing that speaking another's language is always appreciated, Blue Star tried to thank them in Mammal. "Eh-eh-eh," he managed.

Megamaximus Sharkbonker looked at him curiously and then burst out laughing. He laughed so hard that he had to go up to the surface for air.

"Why is he laughing so hard?" Blue Star asked.

"You don't want to know," Superglorious said, shaking his head. "But in the future I'd stick to Fish if I were you." And with that he joined the rest of the squadron as they raced away.

Chapter 13

Meanwhile, our slow journey to the capital of the world's oceans continued. Oceanus is located in a broad basin south of the Bahamas. Cherished for its teaming sea life, warm, clear water, beautiful scenery, and proximity to Disney World, Oceanus draws councilfish from waters as far away as the Antarctic, the Sea of Okhotsk, the Caspian, and even Utah's Great Salt Lake (and does that fish have travel stories to tell).

We paddled over mile after mile of roomy reef condominiums, the lush coral estates of influential lobbyfish, and the stately mansions of Oceanic High Court judges, ministers, and elite entertainerfish, so much in demand at this cosmopolitan, interoceanic crossroads. Some of the wealthier homes had hot tubs, fueled from hot springs that bubbled up from the seabed. Apollo considerately avoided these, knowing that the sight of boiling water would unsettle Lutus. The lobster already had enough on his mind.

The journey seemed to take forever, and not only due to the vast expanse of the capital. We were riding a turtle, you'll recall.

"Maybe you should let me off," Lutus said, giving fresh voice to his frustration. "I'll walk."

"We'd lose you in the first lobster pot," Apollo snorted. "Give me some credit. You have to admit the ride is smooth."

"Yeah, it almost feels like we're not moving at all."

"Well," Apollo said as we reached the top of a coral ridge, "I'm not going to take this back-shell driving any longer."

"And why is that?" Lutus asked sheepishly, ready to apologize.

"Because we've arrived," Apollo said triumphantly, setting down on the crest. "Welcome, Lutus and Petronius, to Oceanus."

The scene before us was breathtaking. To the left

was an enormous pink coral amphitheater large enough, Apollo explained, to hold the full Oceanic Council. The coral grew on the slopes of the crater of a dormant volcano. A gigantic statue of a fish stood before it like a colossus, a net in one outstretched fin and a fisherman's hook in the other. As a sea horse of letters, of course, I recognized the monument to William Shakefish's tragic epic *Halibut*. On the right, across a vast public market, rose an equally impressive stadium of white coral. It was the Oceanic High Court. A modern sculpture before its entrance seemed to consist of billions of small, round flakes, stacked to form a monument in the form of a flat fish. Apollo explained that it honored the founding flounders.

"I've never imagined such riches," Lutus said, looking over the capital of all the world's oceans. "Surely the powerful Oceanic Council can help us."

Apollo said, "One would think so, noble Lutus, but remember that great wealth is more often gained by taking than by giving. And like anything that becomes large, eventually its primary concern becomes to feed itself. Nowhere is this truer than in Oceanus. I'm sure we'll hear many sympathetic words here, but the plight of Higgins Hole may barely rise to the level of today's gossip. Tomorrow we may be forgotten, and eaten, unless Oceanus sees Tacitus as not just a threat to us but to itself as well. That is the key to our success here."

"But surely," I said, echoing Lutus, "Oceanus, with all of this power, can free us of a pack of misfit sharks." I swept my fin over the city. "I mean, just look at this place!"

"Don't be fooled by appearances, noble Petronius. Wealth isn't virtue, and power isn't courage." Apollo sighed. "I suggest that we bypass the courts and appeal directly to the Oceanic Council."

"But surely the courts would rule in our favor," Lutus declared. "We're innocent victims of some very badly behaved sharks."

Apollo shook his head slowly. "My dear Lutus, you'll find that oceanic law is nothing like your compassionate and fair administration of Higgins Hole."

I made a rare admission. "I don't understand."

"I'll try to explain," Apollo began. "Centuries ago, when I was but a wee turtle who rarely stuck my glossy green beak out of my shell, the courts were administered by giant squids. It was a golden age. No offender could look into those big, all-seeing eyes and deny their wrongdoing, for those judges weren't your typical suckers. In those days no criminal could hope to escape from the ten long arms of the law. Yes, we had true justice then. But that was before the sperm whales came."

"Sperm whales?" I asked, immediately intrigued. We'd had many kinds of whales at Higgins Hole, but never a sperm whale, and every sea creature with any education studies the adventures of those legendary beasts. One of them, Big Richard, inspired a tale you may know as *Moby Dick*.

"Yes, Petronius," Apollo answered. "By unfortunate coincidence, the favorite food of sperm whales is giant squids, and though we begged them to spare our beloved judges, they pointed out that the strong have no need of courts, and we had to be content to, so to speak, let whale enough alone. So they ate their fill, driving the few surviving squids into hiding. Now the giant squids live in the deepest, darkest places of the ocean, and we suffer from the mediocrity that replaced them." Apollo sighed. "Despite the justice of our cause, it could take years to get a ruling, and by then Higgins Hole could be a lifeless reef."

"All right, then," Lutus said, "We'll skip the courts and go directly to the council. Let's go at once!"

"One doesn't just crawl into the council chamber, Lutus," Apollo said. "We'll have to apply for a time to speak, and we'll be competing with every fish with a grievance in the world's oceans."

"But surely no one could have a need as urgent as ours," Lutus protested.

Apollo nodded, patting Lutus gently with his flipper. "I'm counting on a friend of mine to help speed things along."

Chapter 14

Apollo brought us to the council entrance and, after explaining what we needed to do, left us while he sought assistance from an old friend, a powerful official in the Oceanic Council.

The reef that housed the Oceanic Council was magnificent. We paused for a moment to admire it. I'd never seen more tasteful architecture, and I stood in awe of the zillions of sea creatures who had built it over nearly as many years. Though they had no names, these creatures, pooling their lives' energies over many generations, had created something beyond the imagination of any named artist.

Even so, it seemed to me that the light played

more brightly upon the waters of Higgins Hole, that our coral had better color, and that our fish looked happier and healthier than those who flitted to and fro before me. As excited as I was to see the capital of the world's oceans, I felt a longing for home, and I felt sorry for these fish, who looked either soft or overworked, depending upon their station.

"I say there," someone said officiously. We turned to see a colorful parrot fish approaching, his tail waggling importantly and his mouth pressed into a tight little hole. "What is your business here, lobster?"

"My name is Lutus. We've summoned the Flying Dolphin Squadron, and we seek a resolution against a band of great white sharks that has invaded our home at Higgins Hole."

"Is it urgent?"

"Everyone I've ever known is about to be eaten," Lutus replied, "if that's what you mean."

"Indeed." The parrot fish arched an eyebrow. "You're named, then?"

"Yes," Lutus said. "As is my colleague, Petronius."

"At your service," I said with a flourish.

"Indeed," said the parrot fish, eyeing me askance, suggesting that few sea horses in Oceanus were so honored. "The case could be quite complex," said the parrot fish. "Did the sharks have a permit?"

"A permit?" Lutus asked in disbelief.

"It's a big gray fish," the clerk explained, "about yea tall and yea wide."

"I'm afraid you don't understand," Lutus said. "These beasts are very unfriendly, and one of them is nearly twenty-five feet long!"

The parrot fish smirked as he shook his head. "There's little we can do here if you haven't inspected their permit. Those sharks may have every right to be at your reef. Everyone's got to eat, right? And twenty-five feet?" The clerk gave a little laugh, covering his mouth in embarrassment as a small bubble popped out. "Great whites rarely grow to be over twenty feet. The only one that ever did is . . ." The parrot fish stopped as Lutus nodded, and slowly the parrot fish's face drained of color. "It can't be!"

"You'd better believe it," I said.

"*Tacitus?*" the parrot fish asked with a high squeak, his eyes as large as saucers. "HERE?"

"Not here," Lutus said. "At least, not yet. I told you he's at Higgins Hole."

"How far away is that?"

"Half a day away by slow turtle." Lutus arched his antennae. "*Very* slow turtle."

"Good heavens!" the parrot fish exclaimed. "Tacitus could be here at any minute!" His eyes grew as round as sand dollars, and he began to dart left and right. "I think the presumption must be that their permit is *not* in order."

"I didn't see one," I said.

"Perhaps they ate it," Lutus suggested to the clerk.

The parrot fish stared back at Lutus with a mixture of horror and disgust. "They ate their *permit?* I've never heard of such a thing!"

"You can see why we seek the council's help," Lutus said reasonably.

"If they'd applied for a permit," I suggested, "wouldn't you have a record of it here?"

"Yes, of course. I'll have to check our micro-fish. There might be some special claws. Oh, dear!" The clerk darted back into the busy reef, crying out, "TACITUS HAS LEFT THE ARCTIC!"

Chapter 15

Apollo sent a messenger to fetch us, and we found our turtle friend at a local eatery, munching on a fine piece of kelp with the minister of oceanic defense, a manatee of long acquaintance named Wallace—Wally to his friends, of which there are many, for it is almost impossible to dislike the minister's breed. I accepted Wally's invitation to sit beside him and tried not to notice when passersby occasionally stopped to gawk at the four of us. Despite the enormous stress we were under, I couldn't resist the temptation to flash a few dazzling smiles, always at home among the beautiful creatures.

As Lutus and I wondered who at Higgins Hole was

being eaten at that very moment, Apollo and Wally caught up on their respective family news, shared recent oceanic gossip, and thoroughly perused the menu, which featured the most extensive kelp list in the city.

"So, Wally," Apollo asked, "how'd you get this job? The last time I saw you, your only worry was dodging motorboats in the Intracoastal Waterway."

Wally laughed. "I was a compromise candidate, someone the two parties could agree on. Politics is all about being in the right place at the right time. . . ."

"Well, right now Tacitus is in the wrong place," Lutus finally interjected. "What can we do about that?"

"If only Big Richard were here," Wally said, referring to the gargantuan white whale I mentioned earlier. "He could frighten off your sharks all by himself."

"And everyone else besides," Apollo added, clearly no friend of squid-eating whales.

"He's vacationing off Australia now," said Wally, a manatee in the know. "I hear he won't be back for another season."

"We need help now," Lutus fretted.

Wally scratched his white, hairless head. "I'm sure we can get authorization to use the Flying Dolphin Squadron, but don't forget the Oceanic Defense

Force. They're the best-trained fish in the sea. You should see them at parade next week. There's a ball afterward. I can get you all an invitation."

Before I could accept, Lutus said, "We have to get back to our friends as soon as we possibly can, Wally. They're in great danger."

Jutting his neck far out of his shell, Apollo thumped his flipper on the table and demanded, "The Oceanic Defense Force may be well trained, but can these fish of yours fight?"

"They haven't been in a tussle for as long as I can remember," the amiable Wally confessed. "You have to admit, Apollo, that aside from the risk of being eaten at any moment, a fish's life is pleasant and peaceful these days."

"Our lives have been anything but peaceful of late," Lutus said. "What will it take to get the Oceanic Council to commit to the defense of Higgins Hole?"

"A good speech," Wally replied. "I'll arrange for you to address the council this afternoon. Don't worry, old friend. Once they learn that Tacitus is nearby, they'll do whatever they have to do. That won't be the end of your troubles, though."

"What do you mean?" Lutus asked, blinking as he looked between Wally and Apollo.

"You're going to have to deal with the general," Wally said.

We asked as one, "Who's that?"

Wally returned an embarrassed smile. "General Finnias J. Trout, Order of the Whale, Legion of the Clam, Doctor of Military Science from Pacific University."

"P.U.?" I asked.

Wally nodded. "You know the expression that a visiting fish starts to stink after three days?"

"Yes."

"I think they had General Trout in mind, but you won't need to wait three days." Wally shook his head. "First things first, though. We need to get you in front of the council. You'll see what I mean soon enough."

Wally was true to his word. Lutus was granted an immediate audience at the council, and we entered the vast chamber filled with awe and trepidation. In the distance, hot, sulfuric gas, a fitting symbol of the ocean's great deliberative body, bubbled from behind the speaker's podium. Vast throngs of fish,

the stalwarts of the Minnow Party, darted among the fingers of coral that ran along the right side of an aisle that divided the Little House from the Big House. On the left, a few dozen fish of considerable proportions lounged in polished clamshells, brandishing expensive seaweed cigars, discussing the newest restaurants, and generally enjoying themselves.

Wally led us to the visitors' gallery, which offered an excellent view of the entire assembly. Below us, we saw Lutus waiting nervously below the podium. Thankfully, he didn't seem to notice the boiling water rising in the background. A far deeper fire seemed to burn inside him.

"Ladies and Gentlefish," the president of the council began, "our esteemed minister of oceanic defense, Wally the Manatee, has just alerted me to a serious threat to our safety. Lutus the Lobster is here to brief us on the situation, and so, without further ado, I give you Lutus." The president, a plump little ocean perch, swam away solemnly while Lutus, with earnest dignity, ascended the podium. We knew that the very survival of Higgins Hole hinged on what he was about to say.

Chapter 16

As the Oceanic Council quieted to hear Lutus speak, conditions at Higgins Hole had deteriorated to a terrible state. I wasn't there, of course, but as I am the reef's historian and poet, everyone subsequently told me of their experiences, which made those trying times as real to me as if I'd been there myself.

Needless to say, when the sharks returned to Higgins Hole and the whales failed to appear, Tacitus's anger exploded into a towering rage, which then simmered into a bitter chowder to which the great whites dreamed of adding tender chunks of fish.

And as if hunger and the constant fear of a sudden, painful death were not enough, the snappers had followed Harry the Herring into his cramped hiding place. "Do that rhyming thing again, Harry," they begged him incessantly. "You're the best!" Harry grumbled hungrily, as did Julius, who floated outside their crevice, watching them with ravenous intent.

Eventually the snappers tired of Harry's sullen silence and ventured to the limits of their cave.

"Hark, a shark!" one of the snappers said. His friends joined him, and for the first time, Harry felt sorry for Julius.

"Hello, shark!"

"Hoping we'll swim out on a lark?"

"Can you see us if it's dark?"

"Woof! Woof!"

"Why'd you do that?"

"Haven't you ever heard a shark bark?"

"Do you think its bark is as bad as its bite?"

"A bite would be a fright!"

The shark growled, "You got that right!"

A snapper stuck up his fins and said, "You want to fight?"

"Yeah," Julius said, "you juicy little tyke."

"What piece of me would you like?"

Julius closed his eyes and, struggling to remember the words, recited:

126

I will eat you head to toe.
Just come out and in you go.
I'll chew fast, and you should know,
it's a rather pleasant way to go.

"Oh, that was cute!" one of the snappers said. "Did you learn that as a baby shark?"

"Yup," Julius said, very pleased with himself as he wagged his tail.

"Oh, brother," Harry groaned. The snappers had made their first inter-species friend.

A few caves away, Miss Tootoo was having a conversation with her own captor, who happened to be Hannibal.

"You know," she said through a thick tangle of razor-sharp coral, water passing noisily through her famished gills, "tuna, when they're hungry enough, have been known to eat sharks."

Hannibal puckered doubtfully. "I've never heard of a tuna eating a shark."

"Oh, yes," Miss Tootoo said as if in a trance, her gaze fixed on Hannibal's substantial body. "I've been thinking about it all day. Ever since I ate my last plinky, in fact."

"I'd like to see you try," he said, looking behind him and pointing at one of his brothers. "Cicero's right over there. Go for it."

"It's a very painful death, you know, to be eaten by a tuna." Miss Tootoo's lips pulled back to reveal several million small teeth. "Nothing quick, like a shark bite." Her eyes flared. "Imagine the pain, Hannibal. My teeth like long needles, starting at your wounded tail, working my way up. . . ." Her eyes grew wider and wider. Soon she was talking to herself, a wild, frenzied look coming over her, her voice rising. "I might feed for weeks on a brute like you. Taking my fill . . . again and again. Gorging myself with fresh . . . juicy . . . shark meat!" Hannibal swam away, casting nervous glances behind him.

Meanwhile, our clever and resourceful Allus Neckus maintained his close surveillance of Tacitus, swimming steadily beneath the giant's belly as Tacitus circled the perimeter of Higgins Hole.

Unlike the rest of us, Allus Neckus didn't start his

life within our protective reef. He harkens from Australia's Great Barrier Reef, a marine paradise as distant and mysterious as the master spy himself. Based on comments from Lutus and Apollo over the years, I have long suspected that Allus Neckus was once involved in high-stakes oceanic espionage, a craft for which he clearly has a natural talent. A secret betrayal resulted in his needing a safe place to hide, and long ago, at Apollo's request, Lutus had invited this distinguished if quirky guest to make Higgins Hole his home. Allus Neckus has lived quietly among us ever since, and it was only now, in our time of greatest need, that we had learned how fortunate we were to have a friend with his specialized skills.

Maintaining his cover, Allus Neckus saw, heard, and smelled all. He was there when Tacitus found the empty plinkery. Countless crabs and clams watched in idle dismay as the big shark cruised overhead. The scent of plankton, which had been so powerful earlier, was fading, the plinky juice carried away by the currents, and Tacitus began to wonder if he'd been wrong about the whales after all. Allus heard the big shark's empty stomach rumbling like the engine of an ocean liner. The other great whites avoided Tacitus as he passed, grumbling to himself as his frustration grew.

"Where are the whales?" Tacitus muttered time and time again. "I can still smell them."

Allus Neckus knew that the monster was nearing his breaking point. Needing to warn Integritus, he waited for an opportune time to steal away undetected. As Tacitus passed Manta Head, Allus Neckus found his chance, slithering behind the coral.

Higgins Hole didn't have much time.

Chapter 17

"Distinguished councilfish," Lutus began bravely. "My home, just half a day from here by very slow turtle, has been invaded by none other than that voracious villain, that scroungy scourge, that shameless shark, the infamous and insatiable Tacitus!"

Several members of the Tuna Party practically fell out of their clamshells. "Is it true?" one of the tunas sputtered. "Tacitus? Here in these waters?"

"Yes," Lutus replied. "I have seen him. I have *spoken* with him. He aims to stay and empty our waters of sea life just as he and his pack have done in the waters of the Arctic."

"We must send the Oceanic Defense Force at once!" another tuna declared hysterically.

"Point of order," a rather intense-looking minnow near the aisle shouted, raising her fin.

The president of the council joined Lutus at the podium. "Ah, yes, Mini Minnow?"

"I would just like to point out, Mr. President, that our esteemed colleagues on the other side of the aisle are proposing that we commit our resources to combat a threat that affects only the larger fish. Everyone knows that great white sharks pose no threat to fish of more appropriate and environmentally friendly dimensions."

"Point of order!" a grouper yelled, swimming forward, his gills rigid with outrage. "Does this young pip mean to divide the council along party lines at this time of great peril? When the dark lord of the sea is but a half day's voyage by turtle away from this very chamber?"

"A very *slow* turtle," Lutus noted, hoping to heighten the council's sense of urgency. Apollo, who was beside me, tensed his jaw, and I heard him mutter something to the effect that Lutus had a long crawl ahead of him.

"We haven't a moment to waste!" cried the big fish.

A grouper rose to address the council. "I move that we send for General Trout at once."

"I second the motion!" cried another large fish.

"We'd also like the Flying Dolphin Squadron," Lutus added hastily.

"So moved!" cried a big flounder.

"Second," someone quickly added.

"Remember Higgins Hole!" cried the members of the Tuna Party.

"The resolution passes," announced the president of the council with a loud whack of his conch shell.

"Point of order! Point of order!" members of the Minnow Party shouted.

Just then, as the council seemed on the verge of chaos, a figure appeared at the end of the center aisle, a fish whose presence was so commanding that every jaw, fin, tail, tentacle, tendril, antenna, and filament stopped at the sight of him. And what a sight he was! His polished scales dazzled like the sun. His gills extended from his neck like epaulets. His every gesture expressed the authority and dignity of the commanding general of the Oceanic Defense Force, for he was, indeed, General Finnias J. Trout.

The Tunas and the Minnows, temporarily caught up by the magnificence of Trout's appearance, applauded wildly as he descended. He looked neither left nor right as he proceeded majestically to the podium, where he joined Lutus. Lutus later told me that the general was much smaller than he appeared to be and, in fact, up close was nothing more than a spectacularly clean trout.

"And you are?" General Trout asked Lutus, the general's nose lifted so high that Lutus couldn't even see his eyes.

"I am Lutus the—"

"I know who you are, lobster. I am General Finnias J. Trout, Commander of the Oceanic Defense Force, Order of the Whale, Legion of the Clam, and Doctor of Military Science from Pacific University."

"On behalf of all the creatures of Higgins Hole, I'd like to thank—"

"I understand that you have a shark infestation," General Finnias J. Trout interrupted, touching his fin to his nose in an affected way.

"Why, yes, we—"

"You are from the provinces, I understand? The so-called"—the general rolled his eyes for the benefit of the council members—"Higgins Hole?" He tittered.

"Yes, that's right. We're—"

"I know perfectly well where it is. Knowledge of

the seafloor is fundamental to military genius."

"—a half day's swim by turtle," Lutus concluded through clenched teeth. General Trout seemed incapable of letting Lutus finish even a simple sentence, and no one likes to be interrupted.

"A half day's swim by turtle?" General Trout repeated, seeming amused. "My good country lobster, I have flying fish at my command that can make such a trip in a matter of minutes. My barracuda and wahoo lancers are on two-minute alert, ready to dart off to wherever I wish." General Trout examined the front and back of his immaculate fin.

"Will you lead them, General?" begged one of the groupers in a voice dripping with adulation. "Will you rid us of this menace?"

The general arched his eyebrow toward the Minnows, for he was known to be disdainful of their politics. This was not surprising, Apollo explained to me in hushed tones, because according to Wally, the general had eaten several of them for lunch. When I noted that General Trout wasn't big enough to belong to the Big House, Apollo drew my attention to the size of the general's ego, which commonly places creatures in company where they might not naturally belong.

After a suspenseful pause and in a voice born for military command, General Trout declared, "I will leave first thing in the morning for Higgins Hole."

Every large fish in the Oceanic Council was immediately on its tail, and the din was deafening.

"This is yet another use of Oceanic Council resources for the benefit of the fat catfish tunas!" Mini Minnow charged. "I say we debate the merits! Is this right for fishdom?" she demanded. As the big fish shouted her down, the Minnows gathered around Mini, applauding and bubbling their congratulations. They had lost to the big fish once again, but they had been heard.

General Trout turned to the president of the council. "As always, I insist on total control of every aspect of the campaign."

"You have the full support of the council," the president replied, staring down one of the radical minnows in the front row.

As Apollo and I made our way down to join Lutus, a sleek gray fish was led before the president, who dutifully recorded the council's resolution on its side. After a whispered suggestion by Apollo, the president quickly added the council's permission to use the Flying Dolphin Squadron. I complimented

Apollo for having the presence of mind to think of it, for I must confess I was overwhelmed in the presence of such power and ceremony. Apollo responded with a friendly but knowing look. "Don't be intimidated. Beneath all the puffery they're no different from anyone else."

"We'll marshal our forces at once," General Trout declared. "I shall rid the oceans of this so-called Tacitus and his scurvy sharks!" Then he swam off to his legions without so much as a word to Lutus. The sleek gray fish bearing the council's resolutions followed General Trout like a shadow.

"There goes a fish with a porpoise," Wally observed.

"He hasn't even asked how many sharks there are," Lutus complained. "How can someone lead if they won't listen?"

"Don't forget about Megamaximus Sharkbonker," Apollo counseled, taking Lutus under his flipper. "We've accomplished what we came here to do. Wally has kindly invited us to stay with him tonight. We'll ride with the general's forces in the morning."

"I do hope Blue Star was able to find Megamaximus," Lutus fretted.

"As do I," agreed Apollo.

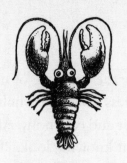

Chapter 18

After a sleepless night, we boarded a sleek manta ray that Wally had kindly sent for us. The ride was wonderfully smooth, and even Apollo marveled at the speed. All around us, the resplendent legions of the Oceanic Defense Force swam with pomp and precision, bands playing, drum fish beating, and plenty of fine food to go around. We saw wahoos by the hundreds, barracuda by the thousands, and smelt by the millions. Colorful starfish cartwheeled across the white, sandy bottom, ready to serve as markers for the legions as they prepared to execute the most complex and demanding maneuvers, many of which had been conceived and developed by none other than General Finnias J. Trout himself.

General Trout pulled alongside us in a spectacular chariot, which consisted of a small, highly polished sea turtle pulled by no less than sixty sea horses. I confess they were somewhat intimidating at first, though upon closer inspection I was less impressed with them. Yes, they were muscular and superbly trained, capable of swimming for days without rest, indomitable of spirit, and all that. And yet in a number of respects they paled in comparison to another sea horse you've met. Only modesty prevents me from identifying him by name. And of course, not one of them could claim to have bitten a great white shark.

While I was silently disapproving of the general's steeds, he was engaged in conversation with Lutus.

"So tell me, General," Lutus said. "What are your plans for—?"

"I assure you," the general sniffed, "that my mind is filled with plans. The appropriate course of action will occur to me as soon as I see the situation at your so-called Higgins Hole. Fear not. You shall soon see the full capabilities of the magnificent forces under my command."

Lutus looked concerned. "Not meaning to detract

in any way from your legions, General, but do you really think these fish can stand up to—?"

"Defeatist! How dare you question the prospects for victory? My cavalry of threshers and makos are feared throughout the seven seas. My barracuda are tenacious, my wahoos the fiercest in the ocean, my razor fish as sharp as they come. My starfish are as resolute as lighthouses, and my herrings have never failed to get out of a pickle. Add my brilliant leadership and you have the recipe for an invincible force." The general grinned. "Do not underestimate the power of leadership in battle, lobster. I dare say, a million minnows under my inspired command would be more than sufficient for this task."

Lutus's antennae drooped. "But how could minnows in any number—?"

"My dear, simple, country lobster, do you really intend to test me on the fine points of military science? Have you never studied the works of Karl von Clausefish? Do you claim to understand the nuances of position, maneuver, terrain, and concentration of bass?" General Trout sighed. "I have neither the time nor the patience to explain these things to you now. Watch and learn, lobster. Watch and learn."

"But, General—"

General Trout drew in his breath to interrupt again, but Lutus reached over with his right claw, his largest, and clamped the general's mouth shut. The general, aghast, struggled to free himself as if he were on a hook, but Lutus held him firmly.

"General," Lutus said, "I'm very sorry to have to do this, but it's for your own good. I'm worried about you and your wonderful fish. Have you ever seen a great white shark? Do you have any idea how awesomely powerful these creatures are? I need to know that you understand what you're up against."

When Lutus relaxed his grip, the angry trout sputtered, "How dare you, you fiend!"

"Please answer my—"

"Of course I've seen great whites," the general blustered.

"I just want to be sure you know what you're in for—"

"Leave everything to me," General Trout said. As he pulled away, we heard him muttering, "Incompetent amateurs . . . conch-shell strategists . . ."

"I hope that puffed-up trout's a tenth as good as he thinks he is," Apollo said to me.

"No leader can succeed who won't listen," Lutus

repeated with a sigh. "I just hope Blue Star has reached Megamaximus Sharkbonker and the Flying Dolphin Squadron."

Carried gracefully by the speedy manta ray, it wasn't long before we began to pass familiar landmarks. The seabed rose beneath us, and the water grew warmer. Soon the shadows of General Trout's mighty legions passed over the white sandy shoals that surrounded Higgins Hole. The manta ray took us directly to General Trout's field headquarters, where we found the newly arrived general strutting around a map lecturing the commanders of his legions.

"I've just received a complete report from one of our eels on the disposition of the so-called great whites," he was saying, tapping the map with his fin as he spoke. "Ten of the sharks are spread inside the pink reef that surrounds Higgins Hole. Their leader, this Tacitus, is floating above an abyss in the center." He stared boldly into their faces. "Leave Tacitus to me," he said. "He's mine."

"Pardon," Lutus said, clearing his throat, "are

you suggesting, General Trout, that you are going to handle Tacitus by yourself?"

Apollo tugged at one of Lutus's back legs. "Lutus," he whispered, "leave this to the general. It's a military matter now. It's out of our hands."

"But I can't just sit here and let him get himself eaten!" Lutus whispered back. "It wouldn't be right—"

"That," General Trout replied in answer to Lutus's original question, "is precisely what I am suggesting. What you fail to grasp, my annoying, provincial bottom-dweller, is the moral element of conflict, the power of the martial spirit, of what we call *élan*. I'm talking about the steel that exists within each of us, the power of pride, the *grrrrr* in greatness, the unstoppable force of self-confidence!"

"How will you use the Flying Dolphin Squadron?" Lutus asked.

"Rank amateurs," General Trout said, brushing a piece of seaweed off his epaulet. "This will all be over by the time they get here, and in any case, they are no match for Tacitus."

I looked to Apollo, wondering if General Trout's assessment of the Flying Dolphin Squadron was correct. We were placing so much hope in them.

"Please don't face Tacitus alone," Lutus begged

the general. "You should be here, directing your commanders, not serving yourself up as an hors d'oeuvre."

The commanders laughed, and none louder than General Finnias J. Trout. "I appreciate your concern for my safety, lobster, but I suggest you find a good viewing place from which you can watch history being made today."

"And what of the other sharks?" Lutus asked.

"What other sharks?"

"Your eel has accounted for only eleven," Lutus said. "We saw at least twenty."

"I assure you our intelligence is reliable," Trout scoffed, growing annoyed by the meddling of this civilian. "Traumatized victims frequently overestimate the strength of their attackers. And if some of the sharks are missing, it's perfectly obvious that Tacitus has sent them off to scout for new hunting grounds."

Several of the commanders nodded enthusiastically, including the newly arrived leaders of the makos and threshers, each as handsome and dashing as you'd expect at the heads of such elite units.

Lutus exchanged a meaningful look with Apollo and then with me. The professionals wouldn't listen.

We'd done our best to warn them. Now we could only hope they knew what they were doing. Lutus said, "I'm not trying to second-guess you, General. Thank you for coming to help us. We're counting on you to save our homes and our lives. We desperately need a victory today."

"Fear not," the general said. "Soon you'll be living your dull little lives in peace and safety."

Lutus looked to the other commanders, fish who would soon risk their lives, and said, "I wish I knew how to properly thank you."

"An impressive statue of me in a prominent place is all the gratitude we require." General Trout smiled with utter confidence. "Return to Higgins Hole. Victory will soon be ours. You have my word."

Chapter 19

It took only a few minutes for Apollo to carry us to the reef's secret entrance: a narrow, winding passage-way barely large enough for a wizened sea turtle and two smallish passengers. Once we were inside, the going was especially slow because the passage was crowded with every manner of fish. Each refugee greeted us with urgent hope, for each was hungry and very afraid. Lutus offered what comfort he could, telling all that the oceanic legions were encamped at the shoals.

The passage widened as it reached the interior of the reef, and there, completely blocking the entrance,

was Miss Tootoo, who, I must confess, appeared thinner after her day in hiding.

"We're back," Lutus called from behind her tail.

"Lutus? Is that you?" She squeezed to the side, and we joined her vantage point. From the mouth of the passage we had a perfect view of Higgins Hole. As General Trout had claimed, Tacitus floated in the center, his long, powerful body relaxed, his eyes closed. It made me shudder just to look at him. Ten great whites cruised in slow circles around the perimeter of the reef, moving a little out of their way when they got near Miss Tootoo, who had obviously unnerved them with her hungry ravings. I have to admit that there was something terrifying in her gaze.

"Lutus!" Apollo whispered excitedly. "Look! It's started."

We strained our necks. At first I didn't see anything, just some starfish resting on the seafloor. Then one of them raised itself on its five arms, moved forward, and plopped back down, motionless. Another followed. Then another. Slowly the starfish sneaked across the sand, taking their assigned positions. Dozens more followed, some large, some small, some blue, some red, some yellow. Each adjusted its position until it was just so.

Together they created a design of remarkable complexity.

"What are they doing?" I asked.

"They're markers," Apollo said. "Watch."

General Trout's crack barracuda were the first to pass through the reef. They were long, pencil-like fish with impressive teeth and fierce, steely eyes. They swam three abreast and with great speed. There were hundreds of them, maybe thousands. They streamed into Higgins Hole and took up positions above the silver starfish, indifferent to the great white sharks that turned to watch them. Some barracuda pointed toward the center of the abyss, where Tacitus calmly waited. Others pointed outward toward the reef and the rest of the sharks.

A trumpet fish sounded two short blasts, and the splendid wahoos charged over the reefs. They swam ten abreast and made menacing formations above the blue starfish, augmenting the flanks of the barracuda.

Then three blasts! The Oceanic Herring Regiment burst forth, swimming to the red starfish by the hundreds of thousands. Soon Higgins Hole was so filled with fish that it was difficult to see across it. Each layer built upon another, rising up in a great

149

tower of fins, teeth, and tails. Gasps could be heard from the nooks and crevices of the reef, where the fish of Higgins Hole looked on with hope and awe, for none of them had ever viewed such an impressive display. When the formation was complete, the citizens of Higgins Hole burst spontaneously into applause.

The trumpet fish blasted again, this time with long, majestic tones, and General Finnias J. Trout pulled up on his chariot, resplendent in his shiny scales, his nose raised regally, his chin jutting out as if to defy any creature to oppose him. The council's porpoise followed, its nose also raised, for it was a proud porpoise of noble purpose.

Tacitus, floating above the abyss, had watched the towering pineapple form in front of him through half-opened eyes. With a slow flick of his tail, he glided smoothly to General Trout, who from our vantage point now looked like a pebble in front of a surfboard.

Neither of them spoke. Tacitus waited calmly, as did General Trout, who to his credit, showed not the slightest sign of fear or discomfort.

Finally, Tacitus said, "And to what do we owe this visit, Trout?"

"That's General Trout to you, sir. General Finnias J. Trout, Commander of the Oceanic Defense Force, Order of the Whale, Legion of the Clam, and Doctor of Military Science from Pacific University."

"Well, well," Tacitus purred. "All of that sounds very prestigious."

"I assure you it is." General Trout sniffed. "In light of your clear strategic disadvantage, I suggest we dispense with further pleasantries. Would you be so kind as to explain your presence here at Higgins Hole?"

"We are here to eat," Tacitus answered.

"Do you have authorization to eat the fish of Higgins Hole?"

"Authorization?"

"Yes, an official permit."

"Hannibal!" Tacitus called out.

Hannibal swam to them.

"Hannibal," Tacitus asked, not taking his eyes from the general, "do we still have that permit?"

"Ah, I think Julius ate it off the coast of Spain," Hannibal replied.

Tacitus said to the general, "Julius ate our permit."

"I thought as much," said General Trout, his nose scrunched distastefully. "By order of the

Oceanic Council, you so-called great white sharks must depart these waters. If you'd like me to pass along a request for a proper feeding permit, I can handle that for you when I return to Oceanus. I happen to know the chief flounder personally, and I could put in a word for you."

Tacitus nodded a few times and asked Julius, "What do you think of flounders?"

Julius made a face. "Too sandy."

"We'll know soon enough," Tacitus said. "General, we accept your invitation to dine at Oceanus, but for now we're going to stay here. I'm expecting whales shortly, and we haven't had one in a while."

"You would openly defy the council's wishes?" the general challenged, straightening further.

Tacitus shrugged. "A shark has to eat."

"Then you leave me no choice but to use force to rout you from these waters."

Tacitus looked at General Trout and then at the pile of fish that strained mightily to hold their intimidating parade formation. "Is this some kind of a joke?"

"I assure you it is not. Your fate, sir, is now sealed." General Trout lifted his fin dramatically. He lowered his nose just enough to see that Tacitus showed no intention of backing down and, with a dramatic flourish, dropped his fin with a snap.

Trumpets blared again, a catchy six-note riff, and the legions smoothly wheeled, forming a solid wall of fish on the far side of Higgins Hole. General Trout rode his chariot before them to loud and enthusiastic cheers, stopping at the center to face Tacitus and his sharks.

"This is your last chance!" General Trout bellowed. "Surrender, or suffer the consequences!"

Tacitus twitched his left fin twice. On his signal, his reserve of ten additional great white sharks advanced from behind the pink reef, bringing his total to twenty, just as we had feared.

I saw General Trout's eyes narrow. We will never know what thoughts passed through his mind at that moment, how this change in the line of battle affected his brilliant calculus. While this failure in intelligence gathering will no doubt be debated for years to come, the general had evidently made up his mind. He issued his fateful order: "CHARGE!"

The left and right flanks rushed in, led by the barracuda, their teeth gleaming in the sun-filled water.

"Form a circle," Tacitus barked to his nervous pack, which quickly gathered around him.

The barracuda shot straight toward them like arrows, nipping the sharks as they streaked past. Even so, many barracuda were badly hurt as the sharks snapped their jaws with savage fury. The barracuda regrouped beyond the pink reef, counting their survivors and their wounds.

"Wahoos!" the general ordered, his voice exuding confidence. "ATTACK!"

The wahoos surged forward, ripping through the circle of sharks with blinding speed, but like the barracuda, taking terrible casualties.

"Herring Regiment!" General Trout called out. "ATTACK!"

Hundreds of thousands of herrings, their voices united in a wild scream that would have inspired terror in many a fish but which had curiously little effect on the great whites, bore down on them uselessly, suffering few injuries because they were simply too small to bite.

The fish of Higgins Hole watched from their hiding places, first with awe, then with confusion, and then with despair as they saw how futile the general's forces were against Tacitus and his sharks. Yet General Trout stood resolutely on his chariot, the heads of his steeds pulling spiritedly at the reins.

154

The general nodded to one of his adjutants and signaled with a fin.

Trumpets blared again.

"SEND IN THE CAVALRY!" General Trout ordered.

From high above and all points of the compass, the threshers and makos charged. We all gaped at the sight of the hundreds of advancing sharks, the threshers with their long, saberlike tails, the makos with their square, powerful jaws.

"Here we go, boys," Tacitus said, showing his first sign of concern. The great whites lined up beside him, fin to fin. A fight ensued unlike anything you've ever imagined. The water was so thick with bubbles and the thrashing of heavy bodies that it would have been impossible to know what was happening but for the battle chatter of the great whites.

"Tacitus, get this mako off my tail!"

"Tally, Julius, I'm on him."

A mako screamed with pain and sank away from the fight.

"There!" Tacitus shouted. "Two threshers are closing on Hannibal."

"I've got them," Julius replied, grunting as he

bumped one of the threshers into a coral reef and then bit the second one.

The howls of pain from the Oceanic Cavalry were loudest wherever Tacitus was engaged, and wounded sharks fell from the fight by the dozens until the commander of the makos was bodily hurled out of the sea and onto a reef.

Soon after that, the battle was over. Terrified, we watched as Tacitus, bearing fresh wounds but seemingly as strong as ever, swam forward in triumph. All eyes turned to General Trout, who stood ramrod straight on his chariot, all of his options expended but that most hateful one, surrender.

General Trout spoke quietly to his staff officers, who shook their heads, indicating that the tide had indeed turned. The facts were clear, and a professional to the core, the general faced them squarely. Though he had fought brilliantly, all the oceanic reserves had now been committed. Tacitus had prevailed. General Trout urged his sea horses onward, stopping before the victor.

"Well fought," General Trout said. "Higgins Hole is yours."

"No, it's not!" protested Harry the Herring, who darted from his hole, swimming in clear sight of the

great whites. "This is our home, and no puffed-up, conceited trout is going to give it away! I don't care how many titles he has."

"But the field is lost," General Trout protested, annoyed that anyone would interrupt his elegant surrender.

"It's not lost until we say so," Miss Tootoo said, struggling past us and swimming boldly toward the sharks, who backed away nervously.

Integritus left the safety of his crevice and joined Miss Tootoo. Though his sail was badly mangled, he held his bill high. Despite all he had suffered, the sailfish's pride and honor burned brightly, and our hearts were lifted when we saw him.

Of course, a finely tuned sense of propriety prevents me from recounting the effect of my own emergence from the coral, but at this point in this narrative the reader can well imagine the impact.

Lutus crawled into full view, followed by Apollo, and soon all the creatures of Higgins Hole were out in the open, congregating by the millions, demanding their lives and their freedom. The sharks were confused, not knowing what to make of this universal display of courage and defiance.

And then something marvelous happened. The

sea was suddenly filled with soft, doleful song. Though it was faint, it was very, very beautiful. Every one of us stopped to listen.

"What's that?" Julius asked.

"That," Tacitus said, his jaws working back and forth excitedly, "is whale song! I was right!"

"Where's it coming from?" Hannibal asked, turning this way and that. The song surrounded us, filling every nook and cranny as it echoed from the reefs.

"I don't know," Tacitus said, making a tight circle to get his bearings. "It can't be too far away. Julius, take half of the pack and swim to the east. Hannibal, take the other half and swim west. Send scouts north and south as you go. Send a signal when you find them. My sharks, the wait is over. Today we feed on whales!"

"Whales!" the sharks repeated excitedly, following Julius and Hannibal into the ocean.

Tacitus turned his attention to General Trout. "We'll deal with Higgins Hole later. As for you, General, return to Oceanus. Tell the council what you have witnessed here today. Tell them that soon Tacitus will swim down the reefs of your great metropolis."

"I'll tell them," General Trout said, his lower lip trembling, "that you are no gentlefish but a savage barbarian, a *whale eater!*"

"If I were to have useless titles after my name as you do, I could choose none better than that," Tacitus said. "Now go."

General Trout, with a sad nod to Lutus, snapped the reins of his sea horses and rode away. We watched him pass Manta Head and the pink reef, and our hopes faded as he disappeared into the darkening sea.

Chapter 20

The shark pack's whale hunt left us a brief respite to contemplate our dismal fate. After General Trout's defeat, our morale had sunk lower than the farthest reaches of the abyss itself. A pack of savage, ravenous shark-beasts had stumbled upon our beloved home. The mighty Oceanic Defense Force had failed to defend us. We hadn't heard a word from Blue Star or the Flying Dolphin Squadron. Moreover, General Trout had assured us that even if they did arrive, they were no match for Tacitus and his great whites. We had progressed from crisis to catastrophe. Now our only choice was to flee or be eaten, which was really no choice at all. We packed our precious belongings and braced for a bleak and uncertain future.

The creatures of Higgins Hole revealed their true stripes that afternoon, each in its own way. Change comes hard, especially when it is forced upon us, and tears flowed freely among the large and the small as they mourned the loss of the lush feeding grounds they were leaving behind and anticipated the rigors of the coming journey.

The jellyfish seemed the most distressed. As they pointed out, the rest of us, after all, could propel ourselves, while they would be left to the mercy of the currents. Tired of their whining, the snappers told them to have thicker skins, and it was I who had to remind the annoying snappers that the jellyfish had none to begin with and that, obviously, showing any backbone was out of the question.

At the other end of the spectrum, the nurse sharks, our beloved ladies of gentle succor, tended to the wounded with little thought to what lay ahead. In their service to others, they found refuge from the worries of tomorrow, setting an example for all who cared to notice.

The snappers, of course, lived only for the present, and amid our despair they were sickeningly

162

cheerful. They laughed and joked, swimming around, singing a song with the refrain, "Eat, drink, and be merry, for tomorrow we fry!" Even Lutus, as he climbed Speaker's Rock to address us for the last time, seemed annoyed with their joviality.

I was talking to Miss Tootoo when the snappers passed, prompting another fish to complain, "If I had a tooth for every time I've heard that stupid song . . ."

"You do," Miss Tootoo snapped at him. "You're a barracuda, after all! Now please be quiet, all of you, and listen to Lutus."

Yes, there was Lutus, standing in his familiar place, his noble profile silhouetted against the silver surface of the sea. But I saw a change in him. The confident cast of his head was gone, as was the straight line of his back. Suddenly he looked his age, and his claws hung low at his side.

Integritus, who had suffered so terribly, swam to Lutus's side, escorted by the valiant Wide-Eyed Three, ignoring as best they could their own wounds from the earlier fight with Tacitus. Their bite marks were fresh and terrible to see.

We all gathered around Speaker's Rock, aware that this would probably be the last time all of us would be together. Silence reigned but for the hush of the waves breaking against the reef tops. As if a heavy, leaden cloud had passed before the sun, the light was gone from Higgins Hole, and for the first time, the water felt cold to me. I shuddered. So many things that had seemed important just days ago didn't seem to matter at all now. I felt a powerful connection to every creature present, whether named or unnamed, and even that distinction seemed unfair to me now. I'll never forget how sad I felt at that moment.

I went to Integritus. "Can we still fight them? Is there a way we can defeat the great whites?"

"I've thought of nothing else since this ordeal began," Integritus said. "I have to confess that I'm at a loss. General Trout's forces were powerless against the great whites, and without the Flying Dolphin Squadron, I don't think we have any choice but to escape with our lives while we still can."

"Fellow fish," Lutus began, capturing our attention in an instant. His voice was strong and steady, but we could tell that his heart was breaking, as was each of ours. We trusted him to know what needed doing, however, and we were prepared to follow wherever he led.

"A week ago," Lutus said, "who would have thought we'd be assembled here today, facing an uncertain future that had until recently seemed so safe, happy, and secure?" He paused, and I heard a multitude of sobs from around the abyss. "I have few words of comfort to offer," Lutus said, "except to say that no matter how dark the present may seem, we are alive, and as long as we are alive, we have the opportunity to regain our happiness. Life demands that of each of us."

"Do we really have to leave?" Miss Tootoo cried, speaking for us all.

"We have to face reality," Lutus replied. "Despite our best efforts and the help of many friends, the great whites are simply too powerful. They'll be back soon. There's no guarantee that the Flying Dolphin Squadron will reach us in time, if indeed they reach us at all, and it's too dangerous to wait." He looked out at us with his dark eyes. "We must leave before Tacitus returns."

"But what about the whale song we heard?" Miss Tootoo reminded everyone. "Even the great whites are no match for a full pod of mature whales. Maybe they'll help us. Maybe it was a sperm whale. Maybe it was Big Richard!"

A barrage of bubbles spread across Higgins Hole as neighbors speculated about the possible return of such popular heroes as Big Richard, Mondo Blue, or the pod of Pacific Ocean killer whales that had gotten terribly lost several seasons ago and stayed with us while their leader recovered from a nervous breakdown.

It was only then that I realized that Lutus was not alone on Speaker's Rock. A small spadefish floated self-consciously at his side, a colorful piece of shell in her dorsal fin. It was the very fish who had first seen Tacitus.

Lutus said, "There are no whales nearby, Miss Tootoo. I just learned that this little spadefish was the singer."

"But that's impossible!" Miss Tootoo cried. "No fish that size could sing like that!"

Lutus gave the spadefish a kind look and nodded. She opened her tiny mouth and began to sing, and the beautiful, lonely sound of her voice silenced us all, for it was indeed the song that we had heard. All of us were moved, for while we knew that it was her lovely song that had tricked the great whites into leaving in search of whales, our final hopes of being saved were dashed.

"I thought that it might distract the sharks," she said, adding, "if only for a little while."

Lutus patted her top fin tenderly. "You saved us all with your song, little one." He turned to the rest of us. "As I said, we have our lives, and we have each other. That's what's important. Be grateful for that, my dear friends. Now go back to your homes. Bring only your most precious items. We must leave within the hour."

Chapter 21

Though Tacitus thought he swam alone, Allus Neckus was never far away, the clever sea snake keeping a close eye on the hungry and dangerous brute. Despite his enormous size, Tacitus moved with easy grace, his long, muscular body gliding effortlessly through the water. But the steady movement of his tail belied the turmoil that brewed in his mind, and he spoke to himself as he swam, not knowing that his private mutterings would make their way through Allus Neckus into our story.

First and foremost, Tacitus was hungry. His stomach ached as if it had been jabbed by a hundred sea urchins. He had missed his pack's last meal, and because the fish of Higgins Hole had resolutely hidden in their holes, Tacitus had not had a decent meal since. The bits of flesh he'd torn from unfortunate members of the Oceanic Defense Force had only increased his appetite. Though he had been dreaming of whale meat, now he could no longer ignore the hunger that gnawed inside his belly. Any fish would do.

The conceited trout from Oceanus had been brave but a fool. The trout's silly pretensions and ornate formations were relics of a bygone era, a legacy of a weak society in the final stages of decay. The fish of these southern waters were powerless before the hardy predators of the Arctic. Tacitus vowed that he would soon eat his fill. No fish in the ocean could match his strength.

The whale song he had heard in Higgins Hole perplexed him. The haunting melody had been faint, so he had assumed the source was beyond the reefs. Though he had promptly dispatched his sharks, he had heard no signals from them in the deep ocean, and he had smelled no baleen. In fact, the whale song had stopped as soon as they left Higgins Hole. Something was wrong. He asked the dark ocean for an explanation, but the seas were silent. Only Allus Neckus heard.

Tacitus talked it through, over and over again. Was it possible? Could one of Lutus's fish, perhaps even Lutus himself, have tricked him? In his hunger and the excitement of his victory over General Trout, had Tacitus allowed himself to be deceived? Had he assumed the whale song was faint because a large mammal was far away, when in fact the source was a small fish close by?

With a furious roar and a violent twist of his powerful body, he turned his nose back toward Higgins Hole. Allus Neckus was so surprised that he narrowly escaped being detected, managing to slither sideways as Tacitus passed.

This time, the big shark bellowed, he would catch Higgins Hole by surprise. He would rip the coral hiding places apart with his mighty jaws, no matter how much it hurt him. This time, he would eat his fill.

Now nothing would stand in his way of his next meal.

Chapter 22

As Blue Star would later recount, at the very moment that Tacitus was turning back with every intent to eat us, Megamaximus Sharkbonker was fast approaching from the opposite direction at the head of the Flying Dolphin Squadron. The eager dolphins churned the water with their strong tails, maintaining strict silence so as not to alert the great whites.

Megamaximus stopped abruptly and signaled to his immediate neighbors that something large was up ahead. His fin signals were quickly passed to the others.

The Flying Dolphin Squadron prepared to attack but relaxed when the Duke and Duchess of Aruba emerged from the deep blue water. Megamaximus

171

greeted them heartily, and the duchess blushed.

The duke nodded to Blue Star, the movement of the whale's enormous head creating waves on the surface. "I see you found the squadron, young marlin."

"Thanks to you," Blue Star replied.

The duke returned his attention to Megamaximus. "We just came across a flying fish bearing news. The good news is that Lutus received authorization to get your help. The bad news is that Tacitus has defeated General Trout's forces. Apparently the brute was about to devour every creature in Higgins Hole when he thought he heard whale song. He's now on the hunt."

Megamaximus frowned. "My good duke, I hope you weren't singing with great white sharks in the area."

For those of you who don't live in the ocean, it's well known that whales are irrepressible singers, especially those of the duke's variety. (I guess that's why they call it the blues.)

"Of course not," the duke replied indignantly. "What do you take us for? A couple of blowhards?"

"I meant no offense," Megamaximus said with a grin. "I'm just trying to put myself in their fins. If it wasn't you, who was it?"

"We don't know," the duchess said. "The flying fish couldn't tell us."

"Perhaps it was just a clever trick," Megamaximus suggested.

"Allus Neckus has been tracking the great whites," the duke said. "Apparently Tacitus is alone, and the rest of the sharks are split into two packs. One is headed east, the other west."

"They've separated. Excellent!" Megamaximus exclaimed. "We'll show no mercy to those whale eaters! I have a feeling some spectacular new titles will be earned by my dolphins today. Squadron, follow me at full speed. To Higgins Hole!"

Whoosh! The dolphins charged after their leader, leaving Blue Star alone with the Duke and Duchess of Aruba.

"Exhausting creatures," the duke muttered.

"Peppy, perhaps?" the duchess said with an adoring wink.

Blue Star asked, "Do you think the squadron can beat them?"

"Oh, yes, I think so," the duke said, nodding confidently, but then hesitating. "Though Tacitus himself may be a different matter. He's no normal shark, I'm afraid, and he seems to only grow stronger each year."

"Dreadful," the duchess said, her mouth curved in an expression of extreme distaste.

"Can you help us?" Blue Star asked, not knowing what was fair to expect from these two magnificent whales.

"Of course we'll help," the duchess said. "That fiend and his mother tried to eat one of my babies, after all, and a whale never forgets. Do you have any babies of your own, young marlin?"

Blue Star quickly answered, "No, Duchess."

"He's still a little young, my dear," the duke said warmly, nudging her with his hairy chin. Turning back to Blue Star, he added, "Don't rush into it, old chap. Plenty of time for that sort of thing."

"A charming young marlin like you will make a wonderful catch," the duchess assured Blue Star.

"A poor choice of words, my dear," the duke noted.

"I didn't mean it that way, for goodness' sake!" Her expression hardened into a look of iron determination. "When you do have babies, Blue Star, you'll understand how we feel about Tacitus."

Blue Star nodded, grateful that he had not gotten on the wrong side of this very strong-willed whale.

"Well," the duchess said, "we'd better get going

if we're going to meet Megamaximus at Higgins Hole. You go ahead, Blue Star. We'll be right behind you."

"It may all be over by the time we get there," the duke said, "but I'd like to see that Tacitus get what he deserves." The duke gave Blue Star an amused look and said, "I understand that you tried to speak Mammal to Megamaximus. Everyone's talking about it."

"Yes," Blue Star said. "I wanted to thank them in their own language, but I think I might have said the wrong thing."

"Well," the duke said, a smile forming on his face, "you made quite an impression."

"Oh?"

"Apparently you told the leader of the Flying Dolphin Squadron that he has very tiny ears."

"Oh, no!" Blue Star looked at the duke in horror, and the duke nodded.

"Dolphins are very sensitive about their ears, you know."

"I'm so embarrassed!"

The duke laughed.

"It's quite all right," the duchess told Blue Star. "Languages can be that way. The important thing is that you tried to be polite. I'm sure Megamaximus took it that way."

"Just remember that the duchess is sensitive about her ears, too," the duke said with a wink.

"I am not!" she protested.

"Well, you shouldn't be. You have such cute little earholes, my dear," the duke said, nuzzling her again.

Blue Star blushed and looked away. He liked these whales very much and wanted them and their offspring to be safe forever. One way or another, they had to stop Tacitus, once and for all.

Chapter 23

Back at Higgins Hole, it was almost time to go. I was with Lutus in his tastefully decorated cave. Lutus cast a final look around, feeling nostalgic, needing to talk. He told me he had lived under this rock for his entire life. Here he had awoken each day to the sweet music of the reef. Here he had savored the wonderfully scented waters of Higgins Hole. Each day he had stepped outside this cave to behold the extraordinary beauty of this tiny piece of ocean we had all been grateful to call home.

"There's something I want to show you," Lutus said.

Curious, I followed him to the very back of the cave, and there, set on a stone, was a thick scroll made of the finest seashells, each bound to the next by finely worked seaweed.

"What's that?" I asked, astounded. Though Lutus and I had spoken every day for as long as I could remember, he had never mentioned this magnificent scroll.

"It's my list of names," Lutus said, unfolding the shells. I saw the names Apollo, Integritus, Harry, and then my own, elegantly scratched into the pearly surfaces. I saw the names of the Wide-Eyed Three and Blue Star. But the scroll continued, seemingly endlessly. There were so many names I couldn't possibly count them.

"Who are these for?" I asked.

"They're for each creature that lives in Higgins Hole," Lutus said sadly. "Over the years I've named them all, every one of them."

"Every creature has a name?" I asked.

"Yes," Lutus said. "My deepest regret is that I didn't let each one know."

"But why?" I asked.

"It seemed like such a big change. I told myself to be patient, that in time we'd all come to believe that

179

everyone should have a name. When that time came, I'd be ready. But I waited too long. Now I've missed my chance."

"I'm proud of my name, of course," I said, "but recently I've been wondering why others didn't deserve one of their own, especially after what we've been through together."

"What a beautiful thing to say." Lutus came to me and put his claw on my side fin, which passes for a shoulder among sea horses. "And here I thought you were a bit of a snob, Petronius. I've never been prouder of you."

"Can we take the scroll with us?" I asked, but I already knew the answer. It was too big for either of us to carry. The scroll of names would have to remain here.

"Lutus," a familiar voice whispered behind us.

We turned and were utterly amazed to see Angie, her normally bright pod wrapped tightly in seaweed. Talk about a fashion disaster! She looked awful!

"Angie!" I cried. "Your pod! What have you done to yourself?"

"I'm on a clandestine mission," Angie explained, looking over her shoulder. "No one can know that I'm here."

I was about to ask what her mission was, but Lutus beat me to it.

"I've come to your home," Angie replied, "to invite you to mine."

Lutus said, "Kind Angie, generous friend, that's so thoughtful of you. But we can't live at those depths. It would be suicide for us even to try."

"Do you trust me?" Angie asked, her eyes fixed upon us.

"Of course we do," Lutus said.

"Then find Integritus and Apollo, and meet me where the abyss turns to black."

"I'll get them," I volunteered.

"Thank you, Petronius," Lutus said, his antennae askew with confusion. "But Angie, how can we enter the abyss? How will we survive?"

"For abysses as well as character," Angie observed, "depth can be deceiving. Soon you'll understand everything."

It's well known that a sea horse with a mission is the most unstoppable force in nature. But this particular sea horse on this particular errand? Even the snappers were quick to move out of my way!

I found Apollo quickly and sent him to Lutus, but Integritus was nowhere to be found. I left no stone unturned, no crack or crevice unchecked. My final stop was the hospital, but he wasn't there, either. In fact, several nurse sharks worried that he seemed more concerned about the safe evacuation of Higgins Hole than he did about his own wounds.

I swam along the reef, inquiring with every creature large and small. No one had seen Integritus. At the plinkery, the clams, who would have to stay behind, were calling out encouragements to one another, things like "It takes a grain of sand to make a pearl" and "Take heart!"

"You don't have hearts, you stupid bivalves," a snapper jeered as a group of them swam overhead.

An irritated clam shouted, "Heart's a state of mind! It's how you feel in your brain!"

"You don't have brains, either!" the snapper howled, enjoying himself enormously.

Eventually I found the object of my search. He was talking quietly to Miss Tootoo, and, indeed, I had been unable to see him all this time because she blocked the way, his once splendid sail now possessing a distinctly lower profile.

"Integritus," I whispered, exhausted from my exertions, "Lutus wants you to meet him where the abyss turns to black. It's urgent!"

"Where the abyss turns to black? Are you sure?" His tone at once conveyed his trust in Lutus and a lifelong fear of the crushing pressure of the abyss's depths. No fish but Angie had ever reached its bottom, and we had all witnessed its nearly deadly effect upon Julius.

"The instructions are from Angie," I told him.

"From Angie?" Miss Tootoo gasped. "Is she here? I saw no light."

Integritus lifted his bill. "I'll go at once. Miss Tootoo, I think we have to assume that Angie's mission, and hence mine, is confidential." He gave her a meaningful look. "You must tell no one, my darling."

"How could I tell anyone?" Miss Tootoo replied. "I'm coming with you."

Chapter 24

Have you ever faced your greatest fear, sustained only by your complete faith in someone else? So it was with each of us, Miss Tootoo, the wounded Integritus, and myself, as we swam deep and unnoticed to the edge of the abyss and then down, down into the darkening water. The light above us turned from silver to light blue to deep blue to gray and, then, finally to black, like a starless night when only the crescent moon casts shadows on the rocks and waves.

Then, just below us, we saw the light of Angie's pod like a beckoning lantern. I looked to Integritus, who nodded bravely, and down we went, the pressure building with each wag of our tails.

"We were about to leave without you," Lutus said, clearly relieved that we had joined them. If he was surprised to see Miss Tootoo, he didn't say anything. "How are you bearing up under this pressure?"

"I feel like I've been entered into a how-many-tunas-can-you-fit-into-a-sunken-ship contest," Miss Tootoo said, "but otherwise I'm fine."

"And you, Petronius?" Lutus kindly inquired.

"I feel fine," I said, though, to be completely honest, I suspect that the pressure at that point would have instantly reduced a typical sea horse to mush.

"Now that we're all here," Lutus said to Angie, "can you tell us what this is all about? We don't have much time before Tacitus returns."

"You'll see soon enough," Angie said, a look of amusement appearing on her ancient black face as she brightened her pod. "I've been looking forward to this day for a very, very long time, my friends. You see, things are sometimes very different from how they appear."

"Whatever do you mean?" Miss Tootoo asked.

"Someone else wants to tell you," Angie answered. "Follow me, all of you, and stay close to my pod."

Mystified by Angie's answer, we followed her deeper. The seconds stretched into minutes, and as the sea pressure continued to build, time seemed to lose all meaning. All that we perceived was Angie's light and the crushing, cold weight of the ocean.

Suddenly Angie stopped and, with a glance back at us, turned the intensity of her pod to full brightness. As we took in the sight before us, we completely forgot about the pressure, the cold, and the darkness. For there, floating gracefully in the inky depths, was a giant white squid of mind-boggling proportions. Never one to exaggerate, I will not hazard a guess as to the length of his tentacles, though one might forgive me for thinking at the time that any one of them might have reached the stars. The white, lustrous creature in front of us would have dwarfed a blue whale. But what I remember most, what I will always remember, were its eyes. The two enormous orbs seemed to see right through me, their piercing gaze holding within them all the wisdom of the ages. They were the eyes of justice. Only then did I make the connection to what Apollo had told us about the giant squids of Oceanus.

"Greetings, Lutus," the creature said, his voice as quiet and deep as distant thunder. He nodded his cone-shaped head to each of us.

"And g-greetings to you," Lutus stammered, blinking as if he could not believe his eyes.

"And welcome, Apollo," the squid added, creases forming at the corners of his eyes. "It's been a long time."

"Is that you?" Apollo said, his voice a mere croak. "Decalimbus?"

"And they say only a whale never forgets," the squid observed. "Yes, old friend, it's me. How many centuries has it been?"

"I thought you'd been eaten," Apollo whispered.

"As you can see, I'm quite well."

Apollo shook his head. "How did you end up here?"

"I was badly injured when the sperm whales came to Oceanus," Decalimbus started to explain.

"I remember that day like it was yesterday," Apollo said.

"I knew I couldn't flee far in my condition, so I found this abyss and filled it with my ink. I hoped visitors would think it was much deeper than it actually is, and my little trick worked until now."

"But what about Julius?" I asked, remembering how the silly shark had nearly been crushed.

"Perhaps I did squeeze him a little too hard,"

Decalimbus admitted, "but he seemed fine afterward."

Lutus turned to Angie. "You've known about Decalimbus all this time?"

She smiled. "He'd be hard to miss down here, don't you think?"

"Angie saved my life, nursing me back to health and letting me share the abyss," Decalimbus said. "Of course, I wasn't quite this big then. I was afraid the sperm whales would come back if they knew I was still alive. Angie's kindly kept my presence a secret, and it's a rare friend indeed who can keep an important secret from other close friends."

"I'm sorry that we haven't met before now," Lutus said, recovering his composure. "But I'm afraid we're about to leave."

"That's why I've revealed myself to you," Decalimbus said, his ten enormous arms floating lightly in the water, limned ghostly white by the light from Angie's pod. "I was rather hoping I could convince you to stay. You've been delightful neighbors. I've watched you all grow up, all but Apollo, that is, and I've grown very fond of you."

Angie agreed. "We don't want you to go. You're our family."

"But we can't fight them," Lutus said.

"They're simply too powerful," Integritus sighed. "Believe me, if there were any other way . . ."

"They won't negotiate," Apollo said. "They don't have to. They simply want to eat us, and they will if we don't escape."

"We can help," Decalimbus said, his eyes unblinking. "We saw how brave you've all been, even after General Trout was beaten. Angie and I think you can save your home if we all work together."

We all looked to one another. If you've ever wondered what joy looks like, I can now tell you. Joy is a little black fish with a light dangling from her forehead and a white squid the size of Cuba telling you that you don't have to leave your home. Our hearts leaped!

Integritus thrust his bill forward. "Tell us what to do, Decalimbus. I'll give my life if it will help!"

Decalimbus looked directly at Miss Tootoo. "I'm sorry," he said. "I know of Integritus and Petronius, but we haven't been introduced."

She raised her head proudly and said, "My name is . . ." She paused. We watched her, dumbfounded, for we had never seen her at a loss for words. "My name is . . . ," she said again.

"Yes?" Decalimbus said, his gaze calm and steady.

She seemed to deflate before our very eyes. "I don't have a name, sir," she said, her eyes downcast. "I named myself, which isn't the way things are done. I'm just a big tuna. That's all."

Decalimbus lifted her chin gently with a tentacle. "I think you're much more than that. It's Miss Tootoo, isn't it?"

I exchanged glances with Lutus and Integritus, for we were all seeing Miss Tootoo in a new light. In the face of mortal danger, we were each being humbled, our pretenses stripped away, our true selves exposed. I vowed silently that she would be Miss Tootoo to me for as long as I lived.

"Can we count on your help, lovely tuna?" Decalimbus asked.

"I would give my life to save our home," she declared, Integritus joining her side.

"Excellent," Decalimbus said to us all. "I will tell you my plan. But first, Petronius, I have a vital mission for you."

"You've picked the right sea horse," I replied.

"Return to your friends. Tell everyone to go to their hiding places immediately. No one should leave. And tell no one about me. Tacitus is returning and he mustn't suspect anything until it's too late."

191

With a nod from Lutus, I rushed upward to spread the warning, the gases in my body expanding rapidly with the decreasing pressure. Within seconds I had completely lost control of my rate of ascent. I rose so fast that I popped through the surface of the sea, flew sixty feet into the air, did three complete flips and a half twist, and plunged back into the water with hardly a bubble.

The snappers were ready with their scorecards: a perfect ten! (Naturally.)

But there was no time to congratulate myself or to accept the well-deserved praise of the many who wished to offer it. "Everyone to your hiding places!" I cried.

Unfortunately, at that moment the pressure caught up with me and I burped.

"You heard him (burp)!" one snapper yelled to another. "Sound the alert (burp)!"

"Don't just float there inert (burp)!" another commanded.

"Lest the sharks our homes usurp (burp)!" cried another.

I was enraged. "If I hear one more chirp (burp)!"

"Hey," one of them asked the others, "what's Petronius's favorite breakfast?"

"We don't know," they replied in unison. "Tell us!"

"Belchin' waffles!"

The snappers laughed hysterically, rearing back on their tails, fins pressed hard against their shaking bellies. Thank goodness Harry the Herring arrived at that moment, or I would have snapped a few snappers on the spot.

"Harry," I urged, "tell everyone to hide. Tacitus will be back any minute."

"And we were so close to escaping," he bemoaned.

"No, you don't understand. Lutus has a plan."

"Lutus has a plan?" Harry's eyes opened wide. "Why didn't you say so?" And off he went, the snappers laughing and belching in his wake.

Chapter 25

Meanwhile, Tacitus and his pack had regrouped outside our reef, and as Allus Neckus informed us later, they were disappointed and angry.

"We're hungry," the sharks complained. "You said there were whales."

"And whose fault is that?" Tacitus growled. "You heard the whale song just as I did."

"You're the one who said it was whale song," Julius said bitterly, keeping his distance from Tacitus. "We just swam our tails off for hours and it was all for nothing."

"I want to EAT!" cried Cicero, throwing a little shark tantrum, as hungry sharks will.

"SILENCE!" Tacitus commanded. "We're great whites from the north, mighty sharks able to bite through a whale's tale in a single chomp. And what have we done? We've allowed these insolent fish to deceive us while they laugh from behind their fragile veils of coral."

"But we were saving room for whales," Julius whimpered.

"Well, there are no whales here now, are there? And since none of you looks particularly appetizing to me, I say let's tear down the reef and fill our bellies with tuna, turtles, and anything else we can find."

"A certain sailfish would be tasty," Hannibal said with an ugly grin.

"I could do with a good lobster," Cicero said to much laughter.

"All right, then," Tacitus said, grinning at them with hundreds of teeth. "It's dinnertime."

The creatures of Higgins Hole returned to their safe havens without hesitation, rumors of a new plan to defeat Tacitus spreading rapidly from mouth to mouth. While I said nothing of Decalimbus (though

195

I was dying to!), the fact that the plan had come from Angie and Lutus filled everyone with confidence and hope, though none of us, including me, knew what was in store.

And then, suddenly, the water began to darken. One minute it was broad daylight in Higgins Hole, and the next it seemed like twilight had come early. The water was filling with black, swirling clouds! All of us, hiding among the coral, shivered in anticipation. Had we been less frightened, we would have noticed that the water was darkening not from above, but from below!

Tacitus charged inside our reef, furious, impatient, and menacing. Thrashing about, seeking his first kill, he finally fixed his evil gaze on a midsize tuna hiding behind an overhang of white, lacy coral. "You'll make a nice appetizer," he growled, not yet noticing the water darkening around him. He closed his massive jaws around the coral overhang, and with a mighty shake of his head, a hunk of coral the size of a large lifeboat tore loose in a thunderous crack. The whole reef shook with the force of it. He tossed the coral aside, his lips torn and bloody. Then his eyes bore into the terrified tuna, who was so frightened that he flipped belly up.

"Not so fast," Miss Tootoo bellowed from behind, "you slimy gray brute!"

Tacitus turned toward her voice, and suddenly he was enveloped in darkness so black that—

"Ink!" Tacitus cried, warning the other sharks, but it was too late. They couldn't see their snouts in front of them. Then, one by one, each was seized by immensely powerful arms, each of Decalimbus's mighty tentacles holding as many as three sharks at once.

"It's a giant squid!" Tacitus warned.

"We can't get loose!" the others cried out in panic. "Help!"

Tacitus was the last to feel a thick band tightening around his body. He bucked and writhed with every ounce of his strength, but he was held in a grip that no living creature could break.

Then, rising out of the murky clouds of ink, we saw Lutus approaching on Apollo's back, Integritus at his side. It was the Lutus of old, joyous, wise, and confident, and even old Apollo swam with jaunty strokes, stopping just in front of Tacitus's nose.

"Hello, Tacitus," Lutus said.

"What is this?" Tacitus replied, squirming helplessly. "Another one of your tricks?"

"It's no trick," Apollo said.

"We're going to give you a last chance to leave," Lutus said. "Will you go?"

"Not until every last one of you is in the belly of a shark, preferably mine," Tacitus snarled, still struggling to free himself.

Lutus shrugged. "Then I'm sorry. He's all yours, Miss Tootoo."

"Open wide," she told Tacitus, her tone that of a mother giving a child a teaspoon of yucky medicine.

Tacitus did what any shark would do, of course, which was to do the exact opposite of what was being asked. He clamped his jaws tightly shut. This was exactly what Decalimbus wanted. With the speed of a magician's hand, Decalimbus wrapped his tentacle around Tacitus's jaw, clamping it firmly shut.

Apollo brought Lutus closer to Tacitus, who, deprived of the use of his mighty jaws, looked pale and beaten. Apollo whispered something to Lutus.

"We've won," Apollo said to the giant squid. "Let Tacitus speak."

"Are you sure?" Decalimbus asked.

Apollo explained, "They wouldn't negotiate

before because we had nothing to trade. All of that has changed now. We can return to diplomacy."

"Tacitus," Decalimbus said sternly, "I'm going to release your mouth, but only if you promise to behave."

"*I'll behave*," Julius managed through his muzzled jaws.

"*Me too*," said Hannibal.

"*This was all his idea*," Cicero added, nodding toward Tacitus.

"*We're hungry*," the others whined.

Tacitus gave them warning glances, but then turned and nodded to Decalimbus, who, after a moment's hesitation, loosened his tentacle, an act of trust that would soon nearly cost us our lives.

"Are you ready to leave?" Lutus asked.

The great beast's glare passed quickly from me to Decalimbus to Apollo to Lutus to Integritus, and I could almost see the plot hatching in his evil brain.

Lutus repeated, "Will you leave us in peace?"

Tacitus lunged forward, his jaws closing around the very space where Apollo's head had been a second before. Though Apollo retreated inside his shell just in time, thanks to countless rounds of Bite the Turtle's Head with the Wide-Eyed Three, the force of Tacitus's closing jaws knocked him sideways. Lutus fell off Apollo's back and surely would have plummeted to the depths of the abyss had he not been caught in the gentle grasp of Decalimbus's tentacle. Unfortunately, this was the very tentacle that had been holding Tacitus.

"NOW YOU WILL ALL DIE!" Tacitus roared, bursting free. Though Tacitus was bruised by Decalimbus's tight grip, his anger and a second chance had revived him, and he was more terrible than ever. "Starting with you, Decalimbus!"

Now, at that instant I thought I heard the faint, distant chirps of dolphins, but I dismissed it at the time as a final, desperate delusion. For though I could see the other great white sharks staring in horror at something approaching from beyond the reef, Tacitus loomed before us in a frenzy of hate and impending violence. Even Decalimbus was helpless before snapping jaws that could crack the keel of a small ship.

"More ink!" Lutus cried.

"I'm all out," Decalimbus replied, showing impressive calm.

Then I heard the chirping again, and this time there was no mistake. It was the battle cry of the Flying Dolphin Squadron!

"Eh-eh-eh!" Megamaximus Sharkbonker cried as the Flying Dolphin Squadron filed through the reef. A mighty cheer rose up from every throat, earning a suave grin and flipper salute from the dashing Megamaximus himself.

"So, Tacitus," Megamaximus said, "we finally meet. Eh-eh-eh!"

"So it's you, Sharkbonker," Tacitus said through bared teeth. The big shark grew calm, which was somehow even more terrifying, for it showed his confidence. "At last."

"Your friends don't look very good," Megamaximus said, tilting his head to the side. "Didn't your mothers ever warn you about squids?"

"It's too bad your mother can't protect you from ME!" Tacitus cried, charging forward, mouth open.

No creature in Higgins Hole moved a single muscle as we watched Megamaximus wait, and wait, and wait a little more until the precise split second that Tacitus reached him. Then, dashing sideways, up, down, and upward again, Megamaximus bonked Tacitus beneath his chin and sent the stunned shark spinning sideways.

"Grab him, Decalimbus!" Megamaximus cried above our joyous cheering.

Decalimbus wasted not an instant, releasing the other sharks so that he could wrap Tacitus in all ten of his tentacles. Tacitus struggled furiously as he regained his wits, but his resistance was pointless. Decalimbus tightened his grasp until Tacitus's eyes bulged and his face turned blue. We watched in silence as Tacitus grew more and more subdued, as helpless as a fish caught in a net.

Decalimbus, taking no chances this time, tightened his grip further and further, until Tacitus grew as limp as a blade of sea grass. The great white shark looked as if he were in a deep sleep, much as Julius had appeared earlier when he had floated up from the depths of the abyss. Only then did the rest of Higgins Hole realize that it was Decalimbus and not the depths that had crushed Julius, and that the white circles we'd seen on him hadn't been from depth poisoning, but from the suckers on the giant squid's tentacles.

The other sharks, now free but on their best behavior, were surrounded by the steely-eyed members of the Flying Dolphin Squadron, and by the droops of their tails, all could see that the sharks had no stomach for a fight they were sure to lose.

Then Blue Star soared over the top of the reefs.

He stopped short when he caught sight of Decalimbus.

"It's all right," Lutus assured him, nodding to the giant squid. "We've just been introduced to an old friend."

Then we heard whale song. This time it wasn't the little spadefish's timid, haunted chanting, but the deep, rich baritone of the duke, who sang:

> *Find peace and joy beneath the waves,*
> *for Decalimbus is one who saves*
> *the just and meek from fear of death*
> *by squeezing bad sharks out of breath.*

The Duke and Duchess of Aruba glided carefully over the pink reef and around Manta Head, stopping above us, where they blocked the sun like the hulls of large ships.

"Good day," the duke said. "Young Blue Star thought we could be of some help, but clearly you're already in good tentacles."

"One further task remains to be performed," Decalimbus replied, bowing his head in greeting. "It's a long journey, if you'll agree to take him."

"It's our duty to the oceans," the duchess said

gravely. "We should have done this years ago."

"We're ready," the duke said.

"But I'll need a good cleaning when I get back," the duchess informed the crabs, who gazed up at her with the determination professionals show when faced with a very big project.

"We'll hold a spot for you," Lutus assured her.

The two whales opened their mouths and Decalimbus lay Tacitus inside, supervised by yours truly, of course. The duke and duchess bowed once to Decalimbus and once to Lutus. Then, with a gentle lifting of their tails, they moved forward in a wide arc, leaving the way they had come.

As they vanished into the distance, Decalimbus passed a fitting sentence, saying, "The wages of cruelty and violence are a cold, lonely heart. Tacitus, you will be frozen in the ice of Antarctica for the rest of time, where you will sleep and never hurt another soul."

A snapper puckered his gills and complained to Harry, "That's not fair. Why just a sole? What about the rest of us?"

Harry looked down at the little red fish and, surprising us all, he laughed. We all joined in. Suddenly the snappers didn't seem so awful after all.

Afterword

Just look at that sun, shining brightly on the waves as they play their soothing music against the pink reef. Look at the peace and plenty that surround us. This, friends, is ocean life as it was meant to be.

Ah! And by splendid coincidence, here comes the very spadefish who started our adventure.

"Hello, little spadefish," I say. She's still sporting that attractive piece of shell in her fin, which I notice many other fish her age are wearing now.

"Hi, Petronius," she replies, waving her pretty fins. She's been in very high spirits since Lutus gave her a pet shark.

"Fetch, Cicero," she cries, throwing a starfish, which he happily retrieves. "Cicero want a plinky?" she asks him. He wags his tail.

Isn't that cute?

You seem surprised about Cicero, but don't be. Freed from the tyranny of Tacitus's bad example, the rest of his pack eagerly agreed to enter the plinky program. Now they're as domesticated as the Wide-Eyed Three. Of course, Julius, Hannibal, and the others are a far simpler bunch, probably a result of living in cold water in their youth, but the children love them, and their presence here does lend Higgins Hole a sort of added distinctiveness.

Jumping conch shells! Is that Angie back already? See how happy she looks? Her light has never shone so brightly. And look who's with her! Decalimbus! My goodness, I've been talking so much that I completely lost track of the time. They must be here for the feast. There's Lutus climbing to the top of Speaker's Rock. The creatures of Higgins Hole are gathering all around him, side by side, fin in claw, tentacle in tendril, a family.

"Dear friends," Lutus begins, "please join me in welcoming back Angie and Decalimbus."

"Is this about the naming?" someone calls out.

206

Lutus waves his claws for silence, but without success. Everyone is so excited.

I scan the crowds, wondering who it will be, hoping it's someone deserving, though, to be honest, after the courage and determination shown by so many during the fight, it could be anyone.

We continue to applaud as Angie and Decalimbus take their places beside Speaker's Rock. Eventually, Decalimbus calls Higgins Hole to order with gentle waves of his outstretched arms.

"Fellow creatures," Decalimbus says, "you've saved your home, and ours. The guilty have been sent away, and old enemies have become new friends."

We cheer again, each knowing how much we owe to the marvelous creature before us.

"We've been discussing how we could best celebrate our good fortune," Decalimbus said, "and we thought perhaps you could help us. Tell us: have we learned anything from the fight for Higgins Hole?"

"I didn't," said one of the snappers loudly. "Did you, Harry?"

"Shhh," Harry admonishes him.

"Me neither," another snapper says.

"Well, I did!" another says proudly.

"Good!" Lutus says, pointing with his claw. "Over

there, Decalimbus. That snapper has something to say."

All eyes turn to the small red fish, who at first seems confused, but when he realizes that he's the center of attention, struts forward. I feel a terrible sense of foreboding. Snappers are, after all, completely unpredictable. All of us—Apollo, Miss Tootoo, Blue Star, Integritus, Decalimbus, Agamemnon, Julius, Hannibal, Achilles, Allus Neckus, Harry, the little spadefish, and Lutus—wait for what is sure to be an embarrassment.

"I learned," the snapper declares, "that it's good to live above a humongous octopus!"

Oh, *brother*.

A hush falls over Higgins Hole, but Lutus begins to clap, which is really more of a clicking sound, and we all get the idea and join in.

"Very good, young snapper," Lutus says, "but count the arms, OK?" We all laugh, especially Decalimbus.

Then Lutus slowly raises his claw.

"Yes, Lutus?" Decalimbus asks.

"I learned something," Lutus says. "It's something I've thought about for a long time, something we can't hide from any longer."

"Tell us, Lutus!" we cry.

"This story has no single hero. We survived Tacitus because we helped one another and because we were helped by friends we didn't even know we had." Lutus paused, and you could have heard a fin drop in Higgins Hole. "Each one of us had a part to play. Each of us stepped in at the precise moment we were needed, even if it was merely to remain brave and calm when circumstances could have made us panic. We all made a difference, whether hammerhead or herring, tuna or turtle, mako or marlin, barracuda or barnacle, clam or conch." Lutus patted the little spadefish at his side. "Each of us has a place here. Each of us counts. Each of us is an important part of Higgins Hole."

"Lutus," Decalimbus said, smiling in that way that squids do, you know, when they sort of pucker up their beaks and suck in their armpits. "I couldn't have said it better myself. May I?"

Lutus bowed. "Please."

"Since anyone can be a precious friend," Decalimbus said, "no matter how large or small, we need to be able to address each other as the unique and special creatures we are. And that's why it's only right that each and every one of us should have . . . a name."

A stunned silence falls over Higgins Hole, but, of course, I know that Lutus and Decalimbus are right. I remember the seashells covered with names that Lutus lovingly created for us over the years. I think of all the creatures that I've wished I could greet by name, if only they had one. My snout quivers with excitement. I'm temporarily at a loss for words. I . . . Well, Lutus was right. This is huge! I have to think. Yes, I've always considered myself progressive, a liberal in the classic sense, the rights of fish and that sort of thing. But a name for everyone? Yikes! It's not as though my whole identify is tied up in being one of the elite few with an actual name. I mean, that would be kind of conceited, wouldn't it? And after all, I still have my looks, my envied tail, my style. . . .

"Sure!" I cry. "Let's give everyone a name!"

Amid wild cheering, Lutus throws his claws upward in celebration and proclaims, "We'll begin at once!" In no time at all, the sea creatures of Higgins Hole form a line in front of Speaker's Rock, and several crabs proudly bring Lutus's scroll of names, setting it before him.

"I name you Stiletto," Lutus tells the first in line, a slender garfish who practically bursts with pride as

she swims away, for no one can now say she's not well heeled.

"I name you Meteor," he tells a flying fish, who streaks off to tell his friends.

The next in line is Miss Tootoo, and I've never seen her so nervous.

"Hello," Lutus says warmly.

"Hello, Lutus," she replies.

"You wouldn't want to be called anything else, would you?" he asks.

"No," she replies, "unless you've already given my name away."

"If I'd done that, Miss Tootoo, Decalimbus would send *me* into the ice floes. You're a heroine of Higgins Hole. Thank you for your courage."

"I'd hug you, if I wasn't a million times your size," she says, touching the corner of her eye with her fin. "You'd be crushed to bits."

"Thank you," Lutus replies, meaning it.

Next in line is the little spadefish who started our tale and then saved us with her miraculous voice. She looks up at Lutus with gleaming eyes, her shell pretty in her fin.

"I name you Nightingale," Lutus says, "for your beautiful song."

Overcome with joy, she gives him a light kiss, and I'm a purple sea snake if he doesn't turn as red as a lobster.

Rising above the happy scene, we can see the long, joyous line, winding across the sandy bottom past colorful beds of coral, past Manta Head, and along our pink reef. The wave tops seem to sing in celebration of this, our most auspicious day. Tonight every creature of Higgins Hole will fall asleep happily repeating a name of his or her very own, and tomorrow we'll wake to introduce ourselves to one another for the first time.

I hope you've enjoyed our story as much as I've enjoyed telling it, and if you happen to be fortunate enough to have a name of your own, think of us and be proud of it. Make it as special as you are.